Heavenly Bliss!

An introduction to an Irish heaven

John O'Connell

Oak Grove Books

About the author:
John O'Connell is a former student of St Columb's College, Derry, and University College Galway. He trained and worked as an accountant in Belfast, before a stress illness interrupted his career. Since leaving accountancy in 1997 he has written several books, *Heavenly Bliss!* being the fifth one published. He has previously written *My Name is John...* (1999), *Love is the Answer: The SDLP, Christianity and the Northern Ireland Conflict* (2002), *The Calling of Sinead* (2003), and *The Hunger File* (2004). He resides in Derry city.

First published in February 2005 by Oak Grove Books:
www.johnoconnell.org

© John O'Connell
All rights reserved.
The moral right of the author has been asserted.

ISBN 0 9537137 4 1

Printed and bound by Antony Rowe Ltd, Eastbourne

All rights reserved. No part of this publication may be reproduced or transmitted in any form or by any means, electronic or mechanical, including photocopy, recording, or any information storage or retrieval system, without permission in writing from the publisher. The book is sold subject to the condition that it shall not, by way of trade or otherwise, be lent, re-sold or otherwise be circulated without the publisher's prior consent in any form of binding or cover other than that in which it is published and without a similar condition including this condition being imposed on the subsequent purchaser.

*For the love of God,
Father, Son and Holy Spirit*

Foreword

Mankind has very diverse views of how heaven is, or at least how it ought to be. My experience tells me that heaven is about happiness, and about living as happy individuals. When people are generally happy there is none of the badness and bitterness that leads to sin and evil.

Heaven is a place where anybody can reside, but happiness comes from a thorough preparation for the afterlife in this life. In other words God intends for us to be happy in this world too, and that many of the things we are doing are taking us away from God and preventing us from being happy.

Capitalism, or escapism, is essentially the greatest threat to happiness defining as it does the purpose of men and women to create wealth, and to work as hard as they can. This leads to competition between nations, cities, regions, and communities and ultimately between individuals. This way is contrary to the ways of Christ who advocated by his example cooperation and a greater sense of community.

I believe that Christianity defines "the way, the truth and the life" (Jn 14:6). I believe that the life in mind is a happy one, and that those who go to the father will be those who have sought to be like Christ in their lives, or to be happy rather than seeking riches or material goods.

We all go through periods when nothing seems to make sense, and when we do things that we are later ashamed of. The fact that I have mentioned Kevin Casey in this book should not be allowed to detract from your enjoyment. He may well have breached every part of the Christian code in his dealings with me, but he is still a human person. All of us need to consult with Christ when dealing with such incidents and people.

In my experience heaven will be fun, and that this life should also have much fun in it. I hope and trust you get some enjoyment from this book and that you will understand the main point: that happiness is, or ought to be, the goal of this life.

John O'Connell

February 2005

Chapter One

It was New Year's Eve, 1989. The dispute with Kevin Casey had raged on for sixteen months at that stage with no end in sight. But that night things began to change and the outcome for me looked decidedly better.

It began with the urgings of a mutual friend who had watched our dispute tear apart our group of friends and acquaintances, and cause friction where it wasn't wanted. He wanted me to approach Casey as our wayward friend strolled around the bar shaking hands with the various friends he had or once had – as a New Year's greeting – which he seemed to be doing with his shoulders slumped and his spirits low.

I took his hand in jest as he held it out to greet someone near the bar counter. He looked at me in amazement as I simply said: 'Happy New Year.' It was after midnight at that point, and we were in 1990, the year in which I died.

Our mutual friend, Fergus, an accountant, appeared over our shoulder and shouted: 'That's right, lads. That's the right thing to do.' Casey looked perturbed.

I looked at Casey, who was tensing up and said, 'That's right. This is what we should have done in the first place. We should have involved someone like Fergus.'

'It would be, only my dabs are in the police station,' Casey said sourly, explaining that the police had taken his fingerprints.

'God love you,' I said, half-sarcastically, half-bemusedly. I was snoring like a pig and sleeping less well after his actions against me. 'If only you had used your fists,' I said.

'What difference would that have made?' he asked dryly.

'You'd have done a lot less damage,' I said assuredly.

I looked at Casey again, his hands were beginning to move about, expressing an emerging anger. 'I don't like this,' he said, as he moved away back into the crowd.

Wait till you see this, I said to myself as I moved over to Mark Durkan, now leader of the SDLP and then aide de camp of John Hume, the Nobel Peace Prize winner.

I struck up a conversation with Mark, as I watched Casey out of the corner of my eye. He was talking to friends at the far end of the lounge. I could see one of them pleading with him to do something and so I was sure that he would be back over to me soon to finish off our conversation.

He moved back in my direction eventually. He was walking much more briskly now, as he seemed to sense some urgency. He kind of baulked as he saw that I was talking to Mark Durkan, the SDLP adversary of his family tradition. I thought he was about to move back again, but his momentum carried him forward. He stretched his hand out to me, and I reciprocated. It was a short, gentle, clasp of hands that signified that he wasn't entirely sure whether what he was doing was the best thing.

'Just say nothing,' I said, sensing that the presence of Mark Durkan would annoy him. The clenching of hands seemed to indicate at the very least that he accepted that he shared the blame of the conflict between us. He wouldn't like Mark Durkan to witness that. Casey was an avid SDLP hater, a party that he hated because his family was a part of the old Nationalist Party tradition, and this party had been defeated heavily by the SDLP. There was a bit of jealousy there and a lot of contempt.

Casey then melted into the background and I had a really enjoyable night after the moment had passed. I had triumphed over him and he had been seen for what he was. He had had to change his mind on this glorious occasion and he looked all the weaker for it. He almost changed his mind as I stood talking to Mark Durkan on the second occasion we had exchanged a handshake.

I was in ecstasy. I had come out on top. Casey had been defeated because he had come to me looking to eat humble pie. The moment had passed and the conflict was over. I could rest now that I had passed the test.

I roared as I came out of the lounge that night. I was over the moon. The conflict with Casey was over and I had triumphed over him. I had taken the initiative and I had strolled up onto the moral high ground.

The years I lived in Belfast had started well, but ended extremely badly. The middle was an unmitigated disaster. In August 1988, almost a year after I left Derry after graduating from university in Galway with so many hopes, I had my nose broken by Kevin Casey, a law graduate and it was not a pleasant experience.

There was an incident outside a local bar that began as a row inside over views expressed on politics. It was a very intense moment when a lot of anger was expressed by both my opponent and me.

It was a needless act of violence, a head-butt that happened when I took my gaze off his face for just an instant and allowed Kevin Casey his moment of debauchery. It had been a hot summer and emotions were running a little ahead of themselves between Casey and me.

Weeks before, this middleclass-boy-cum-delinquent, who like me was a former sixth-form councillor in our year at St Columb's College, was offering me his sister's hand in marriage after I courted her a few times.

Days later, he was arguing with me over the existence of the word 'paradigm', which he felt did not exist. But there was a patronising and offensive nastiness to his argument.

Days after that, he was refused admission to a nightclub near Derry for having fought the previous week, breaking the nose of a doctor's son with a head-butt. I should have realised that night that he was volatile again.

My judgment was impaired by a heavy intake of alcohol during what was a celebratory night. It was a mistake to acknowledge Casey. It was a mistake to argue with him over politics, in what became so loud an exchange that the barmaid asked us to end it several times. I ended it after suggesting a way to end it to the blunt and charged up Casey.

When we got outside, Johnny Waters, Casey's friend and the ambitious but pathetic former chairman of the sixth form council, began to dig deep in finding insults fit for the occasion. As I was about to respond to him, Casey butted in and I unleashed my anger on him.

Casey then assaulted me. Later that night I introduced charges against him with the police.

The following day I met Casey to agree terms for his restitution, and to allow me to withdraw the charges. But I realised then from what he was saying that Casey was not going to play ball. I was not so naïve to expect him to just give up the ghost, but he did say that it was 'a fair cop'. It was a stunning admission of guilt.

He agreed to write a letter, accepting that he was responsible for assaulting me and apologising for his actions. But over the ensuing weeks, he cried and cried his way out of this part of our agreement. He became indignant that he was not to blame and that it was my fault in some indiscernible way.

I switched the terms of our agreement so that he took his letter to three acquaintances who might use their influence on Casey, but he was not to show it to me any more. It was a compromise. But Casey seemed rigid and unable to negotiate.

He had also agreed to pay my expenses in relation to any treatment I may have for my injury, which was not expected to be substantial. I sent him the list of expenses in due course, and on receiving it he erupted that night in the same bar, in what was probably technically another assault on me. It was at least threatening behaviour.

This time he had the sense not to touch me. But I wasn't going to 'get a penny' out of him as he roared into the side of my face like Boris Yeltsin roaring into Michael Gorbachev's face in the Russian parliament in the 1980's. I reintroduced charges then after much thought, in order to protect myself, and recognising that our agreement was null-and-void. He was a man without honour.

The charges were dropped by the DPP after six months. Six months later Casey assaulted me yet again when he grabbed my wrists in a nightclub in county Donegal. But he was learning. He was much miffed at being accused of being a criminal, and him a trainee solicitor. But a criminal was what he was acting like, and he seemed to want to prove it. He let go of my wrists pretty quickly when he realised that I wasn't afraid of him.

But I did fear him in the sense that he was a nutcase, capable of destroying my life in the way that he was destroying his own. Casey was dragged away that night by his own friends like his political colleagues dragged away Ian Paisley after he insulted the Pope in the European parliament. Casey was beaten. I had tamed the beast.

But I was not to know what lay ahead. I was on the ropes after the assault happened. I was no longer my usual self. I was often tense, and I suffered from mild mood changes. I felt the pressure of exams for the first time since I studied for my O'levels in the dim and distant past.

I had a pressured enough first set of exams in May 1988, where I only had to study for Taxation, having been exempted through my studies in Galway from doing the whole four subjects. This was exhausting enough, as it was difficult to motivate yourself in a total sense for just one exam.

I passed that and was through to study for my second set of exams, Professional Three of Institute of Chartered Accountants in Ireland. It was a time for knuckling down again and doing my best to get through those exams.

I studied hard from the end of January onwards for the exams, which were in June 1989. I was tense and rigid at times as I struggled with some of the tougher areas. I felt a level of tension in my body that I had never consciously noticed before in my life.

It was a difficult time in the immediate aftermath of the assault by Kevin Casey. It was always on my mind between late August 1988 and June 1989, a period that covered the entire course of study for the exams.

The tension between doing what I believed to be the right thing and what was in fact a difficult, and at times impracticable, course played on me. It was, of course, right that I did my duty as a Christian and stood up to the bullying of Casey, but I lived in a house in Belfast shared by two Derry lads who were quite friendly with him.

I felt ostracised by my housemates, even if it was never stated as such, at a time when I needed all the good company I could get. Though they were not friends to me or to too many others, it added to the pressure of doing the right thing as opposed to becoming a spineless jelly.

Yet I felt less than a man, in reporting the matter to the police. I had acted like a woman who had been assaulted or raped, even if most women rarely report such matters. I had nevertheless felt like a woman after the night in question. It was a very embarrassing assault rather than a vicious one.

I had to stand up to him, one way or other. If I went down the physical route I would be no better than him, since I knew that I could beat him. There was also the strong possibility that I would face assault charges if I beat him up.

I was advised by several people to take my anger out on him. I was told to get a baseball bat and smack him over the head with it. It was a simple solution that might have quelled my anger from internalising itself. But it might have led to a murder sentence, or even just tit for tat assaults until one of us was disabled or dead.

Nevertheless, my anger was not in relation to being assaulted. That had happened and that was that. My anger was more focussed on my desire to one day follow in my father's footsteps as a politician. I couldn't rise to the heights of politics if I had been assaulted. It showed lack of judgement and lack of character, even if it wasn't my fault.

I wish the former Northern Ireland secretary had been around at that time. John Reid MP came here, having coined the cry: 'Better a broken nose than a bended knee'.

It was entirely appropriate to my circumstances. I had to fight the battle with Casey on the night in question. It was a matter of standing up against a bully and a thug. I couldn't back down. It was better that I received injuries than I backed down and walked away with a jelly spine.

That was the way I always saw things. There was no negotiating with republicans in my youth. They were to be pitied and pilloried. They were 'them' and we were 'us'. There was no room for blurring the distinction while the campaign of violence carried on. With Casey, it was similar.

There was a strong element of petty jealousy present in the run up to the assault when Casey wouldn't accept the veracity of the word 'paradigm'. That petty jealousy was at the heart of the matter.

I was on course to make a name for myself before the Casey incident. But I was also studying for professional exams. The stress and the pressure of the aftermath of the Casey incident made me even more susceptible to the effects of minor mood changes.

I was depressed at times during that period, a period when I should have been celebrating my achievements on the road to qualifying as a chartered accountant. But Casey wouldn't leave it alone. He couldn't. It was beyond him to accept that he had done wrong.

He certainly got his fingers burned by me. The way he came into the New Year's Eve celebrations in Da Vinci's was a revelation. He came with his tail between his legs, the hard-done by local hero who was just doing what seemed right. He couldn't remember being a thug because I had knocked the thug out of him.

He was tamed, harmless, beaten.

But it had taken more out of me than it had him. I had had to change too. I had had to go on a war footing and fight propaganda with propaganda of my own.

I was trapped in a cauldron of pressure with it coming at me from all angles. I had no-one in Belfast close enough to talk about it. I was alone.

Had I survived this period intact I would have been the toughest, most strong-minded person in the history of mankind. It was that serious. I was really full of soul and intensity, the likes of which would have driven me on to great success.

As 1990 passed, I was given the mistaken impression that my troubles were over. I felt as though I had conquered Everest and come through the Amazonian jungle, all at the same time.

But I hadn't. I had been weakened by the uncertainties in the period running up to that, when I didn't know what way certain people would take my stand against that "beast".

I was also to do my final set of exams in August 1990, and I was not finding it easy to do any work for them. In short, I was exhausted and I simply could not raise my game to carry on with the struggle.

In April 1990, things began to change for me. I had to speed my mind up again in order to reach the level of work rate required to make a fair attempt at the course. I didn't really feel comfortable or confident about doing that.

In the past I would have begun a little earlier to get my notes in shape before I would have embarked on more difficult work. In other words, I would have built my work rate up fairly slowly.

What I was actually doing was playing havoc with my mood, such that I was speeding the thinking in my mind up ever so slightly, but gradually, in order to reach the requisite level. I was forcing a mood change from my naturally low winter mood to my more vibrant summer mood.

I was tired and kept falling asleep in front of the fireside almost every night in Belfast, as I tried to rest myself. I thought it was just the heat from the fire, and it could have been, were it not for my lack of effort in my studies.

But I was still struggling on. I was still able to function, especially in Belfast.

Derry was where the problem lay. When I went home, I was reminded of my dispute with Casey. I was too sensitive to any criticism of my handling of it.

I was open to the criticism that I was a ruthless social climber who had shafted a former friend in order to preserve my own reputation. Not only that, but I had almost ended his career in law by making the complaint against him. It was a serious charge, and one that was hard to contradict. But it was not true.

It was typical of this whole dispute that it simply would not rest still and allow me to regain my equilibrium. I was off-balanced by it. I was a typical victim, trying to see if I was in some way responsible. I wasn't, and Casey, self-centred schoolboy that he was, was taking no blame either.

Recently, Kevin Casey, now a practising solicitor, described a client of his as having gone through 'a frenzied, frenetic and almost chaotic period of his life' (Derry Journal, February 12th 2002) in which he committed criminal acts. I wonder was Casey drawing on personal experience in choosing these words. His client was almost the same age as him, when Casey had a similar period in his life.

I was not a card-carrying member of any organisation. I had no axe to grind. I had no chip on my shoulder about any group. I was my own man. I ploughed my own furrow.

I walked out of the office one day in Belfast as D-Day approached. Sean Cavanagh, my boss, was with me.

'Are you going to do something like study to become a priest when you qualify?' Sean asked curiously.

'No way, Sean,' I gulped, taken aback. 'We do more good than they ever did.'

I thought that Sean was relieved by my response. But why did he ask? What prompted him? I had never said any such thing since I met him three years before.

I was not sufficiently conspiratorial to draw any conclusion from his words, but something niggled at me. It wasn't the kind of thing that you ask someone.

My response to him was as an accountant who was involved in job creation in terms of helping to create dozens of jobs all over the North. I was an expert in computer modelling for business plans and preparing financial projections.

The North was particularly violent around that time. People were disgusted by the violence. They were particularly put off by events such as 'the corporals' deaths in West Belfast in 1988, when at a republican funeral, two British army undercover officers were uncovered and killed.

'John, we need another Kennedy,' Dermot, a solicitor friend, had said to me that night after the awful moment, implying that I was that other John F. 'Kennedy'.

'No-one can do it on his own,' I said.

The priests of my parish were also a concern of mine ever since the dispute with Casey had blown up. Casey was close to the Church establishment in Derry since his father was bursar at St Columb's.

One of those priests was Fr Colum Clerkin, a former dean of St Columb's College. His brother, another priest, officiated at the wedding of a friend in April 1990 in the Waterside parish, St Columb's.

'I know of him,' he said, as the groom introduced me. I didn't know how he was aware of me. It could have been just an off-the-cuff comment from a priest pretending to know everyone, or it could have meant more than that.

It could have meant that he was aware of the dispute I had had with Casey, and disapproved of my actions.

It was just a comment, but it unnerved me as Fr James Clerkin was the brother of my parish priest and Casey's.

I wrote to Fr Colum Clerkin in the aftermath of the wedding, suggesting that he should not take all things at face value, and that he should note that there was no level beneath which my enemies would not go. They would go to any lengths.

I suggested that I was 'embarrassed and ashamed' of what happened that night, but that it was not my fault.

It was Easter Sunday shortly after that. I attended mass in a neighbouring parish to avoid eye contact with Fr Clerkin as I was now embarrassed, having written a silly letter to which he had not replied.

'If you are embarrassed …' began the priest in his sermon. I thought nothing of it.

'If you are ashamed …' he continued, with a bounce in his step as if he thought he was walking on water. He seemed elevated, as if he was carrying out orders on behalf of the Church.

'Ashamed' and 'embarrassed', I thought, were very pertinent words at that particular time.

I went to Belfast to think about the words. Could it have been just a coincidence?

Brendan, my housemate, arrived coincidentally from his family home in Portrush on a Sunday night, when he was off the next day, and he would never arrive on a Sunday night. As I went to bed, he made a strange comment.

'Where are you going now?' he asked gently.

'To bed,' I replied, almost confused by his questioning of the obvious.

'Good man,' he said under his breath.

Why did he say that? I asked myself as I went up to bed. Was he worried that I had come up to Belfast to commit suicide? If not, why was I a 'good man'. This implied that I was doing something that didn't seem natural. Should I have been considering suicide?

A woman followed me in the park as I went for a stroll to clear my head the next day. It was strange. As I returned home, another woman from my dim and distant past walked by me. She was with a man and she seemed to be heavily pregnant.

What was going on? There were a lot of coincidences, and they were adding up in my mind. I was calculating that there was something going on. I didn't know what it was, but there just seemed to be something going on.

My doctor hurried me out of his surgery the next morning. He was an SDLP councillor who normally stopped for a chat. He seemed blasé about a lump I had on the side of my stomach.

'I'll cut it out here if it ever gives you any bother,' he said. What did he mean by that? Things were confusing me. There were a couple of old men waiting outside when I left his room. Was he worried about them? Were they republicans making sure that he didn't let the cat out of the bag in relation to the threat against me?

Peter, my closest friend in Belfast, was very agitated at lunch that day. He smoked continuously and kept looking over his shoulder in this dingy café where we had gone for the first time. What was he worried about?

Peter and the SDLP councillor could have been Knights of Columbanus. So could my housemate, Brendan.

I may have also taken on another Knight's son in Derry, and they wouldn't have liked the fact that I had almost ended his legal career. They were out to get me alright, I sensed in the unconscious.

But what was bothering Peter? What bothered the doctor? What was wrong with Brendan?

I asked Brendan first. He said I was becoming paranoid. No, they were definitely out to get me, whether I was becoming paranoid or not.

I was becoming paranoid. The flows of anxiety were hitting me now. I was worried. I went to work the next day. I was agitated at work and scolded by the temporary secretary for invading her territory too much.

Sean left early as usual, but stopped unusually to speak to me before he went.

'How is the course going?' he asked. That was the first time he asked since the previous year's exams.

I thought about it as I walked home. Sean was now acting unusually. It was strange that he had spent substantial parts of the day with the door of his office closed, and talking to a former Sinn Fein councillor and businessman.

I didn't draw the conclusion immediately, but I eventually arrived at the conclusion that Sean could have been covering his tracks in the event of something happening to me. 'I was only talking to him yesterday about the course,' he could have said to the police if something happened to me. Something big was going on.

I panicked. I began to tell another housemate about my troubles. His name was Ian, a Newry post-graduate business student at Queens University. He was confused by my anxious words. He couldn't think of any reason for me being afraid.

I was becoming even more afraid as I remembered that the IRA had murdered a man they'd accused of being an informer earlier that week in Newry. Perhaps it was a killing to prepare the way for another killing, to make the second seem reasonable because the first was perceived as such.

Then I had a real panic attack as I recalled that I had had a Belfast woman back in my room the previous Thursday. She was from Ballymurphy, where Gerry Adams held the sway for years as the local IRA commander. She even told me that she was 'IRA' in a believable fashion.

Was I fucked now? She was IRA. She could have been making observations about the house before an attack. The

Knights and the IRA were ganging up on me. There was some kind of conspiracy. It couldn't have been just coincidences.

I rang the RUC. They came out. They didn't believe my story, but they went away to check with Special Branch. It was more urgent than that. It was very urgent. An attack was imminent.

BAMP, bamp, BAMP, Bamp. I heard the noise of a car horn outside. They were there. I barricaded myself into my room. I came out hours later after the police arrived back, my father having called them, and I sat for hours in the cop shop.

I was calm in the morning. But I went home to Derry with my sister and brother, who my friend Brian had driven up to Belfast.

I checked out the threat with now SDLP leader, Mark Durkan, and he went away to check with the IRA.

I went out that night. The bar filled up suddenly with a rough crowd, and I was fearful that there was going to be a shooting.

'They're going to shoot you dead,' Brian said, when he returned from a long visit to 'the toilet'. I laughed. I was not afraid of death.

Nothing happened, but what the fuck was going on? I was told that they were going to shoot me dead. The IRA were ganging up on me.

My mood was becoming unstable. I was beginning to hallucinate over the course of the next few days. I was hearing things and seeing things that simply could not be. I was becoming unwell, and yet I felt so well.

Apart from the momentary sensations of anxiety, and the paranoia, I was alright.

I was triumphant at the attention that I was receiving at the hands of the Knights and the IRA. I was jubilant as I had beaten them when they had to resort to such methods. They were a bunch of cowards ganging up on one person, and they had lost.

I have no doubt that they wanted me to die. I have no doubt that they wanted to kill me. My friend Brian had said that they we going to shoot me.

But why would they be so determined? The answer to that is simple. I was a potential successor to John Hume. I was about to become a qualified accountant and I was well positioned to throw my hat into the ring politically when the time was right.

There were those who openly thought of me as the next John Hume. They spoke of me in glowing terms before the Casey incident as an obvious political successor to the local and European MP. There were eager eyes watching my rise through the ranks of society from my days at St Columb's, and there were jealous eyes in some camps.

I always said that if there were better men or women than me that I would let them go ahead since I was fully aware that politics was not an easy career. But certain people believed that I should not have that option.

Sinn Fein was their party in terms of values. They didn't like to admit it publicly, but there were many of them who believed that the IRA cause was a just one. The only problem with Sinn Fein was that it was a party that came from the underclass, and they would have no truck with being led by the poor. Sinn Fein were 'scum' as Kevin Casey had said to me.

Sinn Fein were too radical, too communistic, and too poor for the well-heeled Knights of Columbanus. They wanted their own party, and it would not be a social democratic party. They wanted their old Nationalist conservative party back. They lamented its loss.

I may have been a direct threat to their plans. They had to stop me. I had given them the opportunity by defeating Kevin Casey and they didn't like it one little bit. It was considered a political move to use the RUC and so I had broken their rules, and they were going to teach me a lesson.

The only option I had now that the considerable power of the IRA and the Knights of Columbanus were opposing me was to become ill. It was only logical. It made it impossible for them to kill me, or so I thought.

I was a formidable opponent. In Spring 1986, I had uncovered the secret code that lay waiting to be broken for almost 2,000 years, which declared that the leader of Sinn Fein was the Antichrist.

The Church seemed out of favour with God, God choosing a fervent supporter of a political party and not an innocent member of the local Church for his revelation. Later, other things seemed to confirm an indifference at least to the Church hierarchy. The great decade of scandals in the Church when, in the 1990's, God seemed to desert them, and there was paedophile priest after paedophile priest, and scandals involving bishops.

One bishop in particular summed up the nature of God's hostility to the Church hierarchy. It firmly related to my predicament. That was the scandal involving the Bishop of Galway. His name was Eamon Casey, the blasé Bishop of my former diocese who drove so recklessly they wrote a song about him, and who shamed everyone in the Church.

While I was a student he came to my attention one Sunday when he wrote a pastoral letter condemning the ills of underage drinking. I thought it was a valid interjection until I heard in the news the following week that he was convicted of drink-driving whilst driving out of a red light district in London.

He went to court in civilian clothes to plead guilty, and was duly found out. So began the tirade of abuse against the Catholic faithful, including me, in the parishes around Galway. He was a hypocrite.

Later he was uncovered as the father of a young man after having had a sexual relationship with a friend years earlier. He was a double hypocrite. The whole Catholic Church in Ireland was in the hothouse where abuse and ridicule were the order of the day.

But Casey was Casey. Bishop Casey was Kevin Casey. He would never admit to doing wrong.

The Casey name will go down as the greatest embarrassment in the history of the Irish Catholic Church. But somehow, I feel, there will be even more scandals revealed involving that name. What would we do without them?

I rang a priest in the midst of my fears about an IRA threat. I knew that the priest was best placed to find out if a threat existed. It was often stated that every parish priest knew the identity of his local IRA commander. My choice of priest was someone I thought would know.

Fr Colum Clerkin, the brother of the celebrant of my friend's wedding, was very coy to me about any threat. In fact, he simply listened to my outpourings over the course of a couple of days when we had several short meetings in our home.

'You plough your own furrow,' he said, after those first meetings. 'Isn't that right, John?'

He seemed to accept that I was under threat and that threat involved the suspicion that I might not be ploughing my own furrow. That meant that I was suspected of being an agent on behalf of the British, or the Special Branch, or the RUC. It was as simple as that.

Fr Clerkin prepared my parents to take me into hospital while he was in our home. The moment came when I was so affected by the stress of the situation that I was taken to a psychiatric hospital.

There I was in the hands of God, quite literally. It was fun to begin with.

My consultant was another possible Knight of Columbanus. He asked curious questions at our first meeting.

'Why did you go to Galway?' he asked.

'Why did you study commerce?' he asked.

'I wanted to be a politician,' I replied.

'You haven't got the grades,' he said. He seemed to think that he knew a lot about me for someone who had not spoken to anyone about me at that stage.

'There was a trip to London,' the nurse interjected. The nurse was definitely an IRA member.

He was referring to an interview I had attended at the National Audit Office in London, a British government agency that audited government departments. It was a day of interviews and tests and I really didn't want to leave Ireland.

This seemed to be the height of the Knights' interest in me. They wanted to be sure that they let me know that they were aware of my indiscretions in not defending Ireland and the Catholic Church.

But I was distracted by other things at that moment. There was a stream of coincidences that led me to believe that God was with me in the psychiatric hospital.

Coincidences are a funny commodity. They can be the product of an overactive mind, seeing and connecting events in a very irrational way. However, I was sure that these coincidences were not of that kind.

They were too personal, and they showed an extremely detailed and intimate knowledge of my life. My whole life passed before me in coincidences. Every view that I ever held was examined by the coincidental words of those around me, and on television.

Then Cardinal Tomas O'Fiaich died. He was aged 66 years and 6 months exactly, giving the coincidence of the three sixes. He died while I was out on my first weekend leave from the hospital in early May 1990.

I was numbed. Something was happening to me and I didn't understand it.

Chapter Two

I was dead. I did not know when or how it happened but I was dead. Dead as a dodo. I had suffered from the greatest preoccupation that mankind has, and I was dead. It was as simple as that.

I was surrounded by angels. I didn't know that they were angels at first but over time I began to realise that that is just what they were. I seemed to have entered some kind of zone where things happened. I wasn't sure at first what was happening but from observation it seemed that people were chosen or they were not.

This was it, I cried to myself. I was now going to be chosen or not depending on whether the angels thought I was a good or bad person.

It seemed like a large airport terminal in the spirit world where there were loads of people arriving by the minute and thousands departing in great waves to their eventual destination either in heaven or in hell. Well, that's what I assumed.

I didn't know what way they were going to judge me but it seemed to make sense that they would interrogate me about my life.

'Jesus!' I yelped. 'They're going to ask me to account for every bloody sin that I committed during my life.'

Yet I had hardly had a chance to sin that much during my short life. I was twenty-four, and I was as innocent as they get at that age. Yet I had committed some awful sins.

The worst sin was probably sleeping with young women outside marriage. I had participated in that sin on a number of occasions and I had a feeling that it wouldn't go down well with God when I met him. It was a terrible thought. I was fearful that God would have it in for me if he was that way inclined.

If he wanted to have it in for me then I was fucked. I had not only had sex with young women, I had scared the wits out of one girl one night in Galway. She had trusted me to see her home that fateful night, and I had invited her home with me. She only came on the basis that there would be no hanky-panky.

The first thing she saw on arriving in our living-room was a bed stretched out at the far end of the large room where one of the owner's sons had established a nest for himself despite our best efforts to stop him.

She ran then and I had to go after her to ensure that the excitable young lady got to her home. She ran like the wind, breezing away from me through the narrow Galway streets and back to the centre of town. I caught her in the town centre and asked her to come with me to Supermacs, the fast-food outlet, so that she could settle down.

But she was unstable, scaring me a little as I sat there with her demolishing a burger that was my substitute for a little bit of hanky panky. But I really loved her. She was absolutely beautiful in looks, tall and slim too.

She was the perfect catch, only she had had a bad experience. That was obvious. She didn't trust men, even if she came to like me as the night progressed. But I was too shocked by her initial reaction to the living-room to want to begin a relationship with her. It was a damage-limitation exercise for me for the remainder of our time together. I just wanted to ensure that she got home safely.

But I was not always such a gentleman. I liked sex just like the next man. I tried it on with numerous women. One nurse asked me if I would be as forward if it was my sister I was prodding. It was a cutting question. It hit the nail on the head. I had only days before suggested to my friends that we would not like our sisters to be afflicted by the attitude we had to women.

I had to tell the nurse that she was right. I wouldn't like it if it were my sister's knickers some man was trying to get into. We lay together and embraced and I thought that that was the night over. But the nurse had something else in store for me.

She opened my belt, then my jeans, pulled down my fly and pants, and then proceeded to give me a hand job. I could sense – and hear - her insides erupt into ecstasy at this. It seemed that she had only been testing me, so that she could tell me that I was a hypocrite when I wouldn't let her go ahead, and found it deeply pleasurable to find that I let her go all the way.

I was pleased at the thought that she got pleasure from me. God might take that into account, and I might get to heaven as a result. But then there were other moments when God would not be too keen on me.

There was the Aran island woman – at least she told me that she was from the Aran islands – who wanted so much sex that I could barely perform with her. I doubted that she was from the Aran islands because I believed that she was staying in a bed and breakfast house called "The Aran Islands" and she didn't want to reveal where she was really from.

But I only picked her up for a night of sex. I met her at a nightclub in Salthill, and she and her friend sat chatting with my friends and me. She was rancid, ugly as they come, and a lot older than me. I wouldn't have given her a second look only she was available in the sexual sense. I knew that as I had rubbed the insides of her thighs and she had responded with encouragement by opening her legs and letting me rub even deeper into the realms of the usually untouched. We did this together underneath the table we were sitting at and I knew that she on for sex.

I asked her to go shortly afterwards, and she left with me without argument. So we arrived by taxi back at my house on the university side of Salthill. I attempted to make her a cup of tea but she was disgusted by the cups I attempted to use, which were stained with dirt, and the fact that our kitchen was absolutely upside down.

So it was straight to bed. She took off her clothes as soon as I closed the door behind me, and lay with her legs apart waiting for my body to lie on top of her. God would surely not blame me for wanting to finish the job. And I finished the job alright, with a passion at first but with the knowledge that she was the wrong woman for me.

She wanted more and more until she was persuaded by my lack of action to take things into her own hands. I think that she wanted some young buck from the university to do a job on her and give her a child. Her husband was probably – well, had to be – some dirty old farmer who didn't know how to give her a good time and had not given her any children yet. So she had gone out to get her own.

So God would see that it was her fault. She was the one who wanted sex most and she was older than me and more cunning. God would know all these things and he would see to it that I was not blamed for my participation in the unruly night's festivities.

But what if a child had emerged from the night. What if the Aran woman had got pregnant, and there was a child that I didn't know belonged to me. I should really have been told but I didn't leave any forwarding address with the woman. God would know, however, and I might be truly fucked. It was an awful thought that any child of mine could have been brought up by that hag.

Then again, she was a shrewd woman and she would have taught the child about business and he might have made it to university in time and made a big contribution to society. God would not be too concerned if that turned out to be the case.

But then I remembered that I had seen the Aran woman once again while I was at university in Galway. She was coming out of a fast food outlet when I noticed her, and I recalled that she was slightly overweight as she had been six months before, but she was definitely not pregnant. I felt relieved at that memory, as if a burden had been lifted off my shoulders. God would surely not have wanted a child for me in those circumstances.

I felt that things were looking better again, and that I might get the trip to heaven.

Then I looked and there before me was a woman I had met in Belfast just weeks before I went to my death. Her face passed through my memory as if real and set itself down in front of me so that I couldn't take my eyes off her.

What did she want?

Then I recalled that she had been the best sex partner that I had ever had. I met her at the end of a night in Pips International niteclub when she seemed simply to bump into me as I was about to leave. I didn't even ask her to dance. I just asked her if she wanted to go home with me.

She knew what the routine was. She had been there before to the extent that when I tried to kiss her in my living-room, she asked me if I could take her to the bedroom. The action was going to take place there if there was going to be some action.

She stripped herself off very quickly and lay on the bed with her legs stretched open. She wanted sex straight away. There were to be no soft moments beforehand, no foreplay that might have meant that we actually had feelings for each other when we had sex.

It was *wham-bam-thank-you-mam* stuff, only I was the one who was supplying the entertainment. She was a funny little fucker, in the truest sense of the phrase. She expected me to perform for her, as if I had just volunteered for something by asking her to my place.

She was a little west Belfast woman, who had republican connections. At least she told me she had republican connections. But it was pretty obvious that she was her own woman, an individual and a "liberated" human being.

I laughed at the very thought of this little woman being liberated. There she was taking my juices and she could have caught anything or got pregnant, and she didn't seem to think that there was a problem. She could have got Aids having unprotected sex, and how was she going to explain that to her children.

She wanted me to go down on her so she pressed my shoulders in the downward direction. I had never been there before so I went down and played with her with my fingers.

'You're not doing that right,' she moaned. I fingered her a little more, but more gently, and she began to moan again, this time in ecstasy. She thought I was really giving her tongue when I wouldn't have touched her with anything other than the long cannon.

What would God think of me? I could have caught something from her as she was obviously far more sexually active than I was.

I thought for a moment. I could have died from whatever she had given me. It couldn't have been Aids as that would have taken a long time, perhaps several years. But it could have been syphilis. I could have gone mad and then died as a result of the syphilis she had given me, as so many others had done over the years. That was how it affected people.

What would God think of that? He would know how I died and he would be able to assess my level of fitness for the kingdom of God from that scenario. It was a terrifying thought. I might have taken the poison from a little west Belfast woman and I might have to explain that to God. And yet God would have already known how that had happened.

God would know that after many weeks of sitting in my digs in Belfast, I would have got a call from a friend and we would have gone in search of that elusive sexually active woman. I might have found one and taken her home with me. I would have sought pleasure with her in the desire to escape the pressures of my life as a young accountant.

God would understand my predicament. He would understand that our society created such problems by letting us take on so much pressure.

Ultimately it was a symptom of the human condition. To want to do everything, and to want to know how everything feels before we die is perfectly natural. But it is a sign that we are weak and vulnerable to suggestion. We are particularly vulnerable to the suggestion that the grass is greener on the other side of the fence.

We are weak because we will break the rules from time to time to alleviate the sense of uncertainty and to relieve the feeling of the need to know what it's like to be a fully involved citizen.

Sex was our ultimate weakness. It was my weakness, my blind spot beyond which I could not see. I needed to have sexual relations once in a while. If I could have it every day, like some of the young people I knew, then I would be very happy to do that.

But I liked convention, and I preferred to be married if I was going to have it every day. If I was going to have it once in a while with different women then part of the romance was that it was done while unmarried.

God would understand the nuances of that. He would understand that I lived – like so many around me – in a situation that wasn't suited to relationships and commitment. I lived in a world where relationships were a burden that we simply could not afford, and commitment was shunned like the black plague because it would drag us into reverse gear.

We were young and we simply had not been taught about love. We had learned about sexual relations on a piecemeal basis. We knew how to fuck – at least some of us knew – and we knew how to chat up a girl for a single night of passion. But we didn't know how to look for wives. We didn't know how to look for partners who would be with us for the long-term.

God would understand our needs. He would understand that the one-night-stand was the best expression of love that we could manage in our circumstances. He would understand that our circumstances dictated – from the fact that we had little money to the fact that we had no time - that we live a lonely existence most of the time.

Yet again, it was written that we should "seek first the kingdom of God". We weren't doing that, but who was? Our society was not focussed on seeking first the kingdom of God. It was focussed on the maximisation of wealth, and we were part of that from our first day at school to the latter days of my life when I had attempted to qualify as an accountant. We were part of it but we were not the ones who controlled it. That was done at an altogether higher level.

Under the surface Christ existed in our lives, but only in a profoundly deep sense or not at all. And yet all human beings had a chance to love, and Christ was present whenever there was love.

There was little love in my life when I died. I had the usual desires to be involved with one or two girls, and simply hoped that they would remain single until I was available. That was to be after my study was finished and I began to earn a reasonable salary.

I loved my family at home in Derry and my friends both in Derry and Belfast, but I was growing away from them, and they were not going to feature as much in my life as I would have liked. Casey was driving me away from Derry at the time just before my death.

What would Casey think of my death?

He might be relieved that I had died and was going to leave him alone now after humiliating him the previous Christmas when he had shaken hands with me a couple of times. He might have been relieved that the whole matter of him having head-butted me, and caused me to become ill in time, was now going to be forgotten about.

Would it be forgotten? Or would it become a matter for the police to investigate now that there was a definitive victim?

After all, I had died for some reason. Something had to have happened for me to die. Perhaps I had died from a brain tumour that had developed after I had received the head injury. It was possible but not very likely.

It didn't seem in any case that I had died from a brain tumour. I would have felt something. I would have noticed some of the symptoms. And yet I had become unwell, and was admitted to hospital, before I died so I must have felt something was happening to me.

I may well have been feeling the effects of some kind of trauma to the brain on my admission to hospital, and it may well have been the case that Casey had in effect killed me. But did he intend to kill me when he pulled his head back and stuck it into my face?

That was the question that needed an answer? Was he of a mind to kill me? The answer to that question was that he was of a mind to kill me since he used a weapon – his head – so powerful that one blow could kill a man.

And yet the question was not whether he was of a mind to kill me. If you assaulted a man with a heart condition and he dropped dead as a result of the assault, you would have to serve a mandatory murder sentence. There would be no choice for the judge in the matter.

So if you hit someone with a weakness that meant that they could go mad with a tumour in the head after being injured, or that he would suffer from mental illness, then you are not exempted from blame simply because you were not aware of his or her weakness.

The law was an ass, of course. It would always go for the superficial approach rather than any other approach that might reveal a level of understanding of what the victims of crime have to put up with.

So Casey might be prosecuted. He should have been prosecuted without hesitation but for the fact that the system only takes on a few cases of assault – the very worst of them – in order to send out signals that assault was wrong. It does not deal with every case of assault as it does not deal with every case of rape.

So Casey might very well be worried now that I was gone. It all hinged on how I died. It all depended on whether I had died from a brain tumour.

It could of course have been a brain haemorrhage, and thus would have for all the same reasons that I mentioned in relation to the brain tumour the same potential for causing Casey problems.

I needed to find out how I died. That was the answer.

Chapter Three

I thought about my desire to find out how I died and for a moment I didn't really know what I was supposed to do. Then it hit me. I would just ask someone.

That was easier said than done. I got up and walked over to a man and attempted to ask him where I would find the answer to my question.

'Do you know where I would go to find out if I was murdered?' I asked. The man looked at me in disgust as if I had just asked him to take his clothes off and bend over. He grunted and made his way forward into a pack of people and they began to talk. I thought they were talking about me.

A woman who overheard our conversation, or lack of it, then approached me to tell me that it wasn't the done thing to ask about things like that.

'Why?' I asked.

'You may be on your way to paradise,' she replied, 'and in paradise there are no answers sought to questions like that.'

'But I need to know – purely out of curiosity, you know,' I said. 'I'll be damned if anyone will stop me from learning the truth about my own death.'

'You might be damned if you do find out the truth,' she said. 'That's what I'm trying to tell you.'

'How?' I asked. 'That can't be right.'

The woman was tall and elegant and spoke with a beautiful Irish brogue, the likes of which you only usually heard on television, and at that, only on the RTE News. She looked at me, aghast at what I was saying. 'You might be letting the cat out of the bag on how you see your judgement going.'

'How am I to know how I died?' I asked again. 'I died a young man, you see, and I need to know if it was intended to be.'

'You're wondering if you were called to God,' she asked, 'or if your death was as a result of the evil of someone else.'
'Yes.'
'Well, wait and see,' she said. 'In time you will learn that that is not as important as you think, and that there can really only be your interpretation to the answering of that question.'
'My interpretation?' I wondered.
'Yes,' she said. 'Neither God nor the angels really get into that sort of thing. It's not considered to be important enough.'
'Not important enough?' I roared. 'How the hell is God supposed to judge the man who's committed this terrible sin against me? How is he to be punished?'
The woman smiled. She was gloriously beautiful in her white dress and her tanned skin with its considerable dosage of freckles. 'You don't know?' she asked.
'Know what?' I asked.
She laughed. 'Do you not know that mankind is a self-judging entity? Did you not realise that all sins are responded to by a mechanism built into the human being?'
'Whaaaaat!' I was horrified. 'Are you telling me that the person's body will correct his behaviour if he has sinned.'
'Yes,' She said quietly. 'Not only that, but his body will punish him eventually when the sin has threaded its way through his consciousness, and caused him to feel guilty.'
'But some people have no consciences,' I countered. 'They can do as they please and get away with it, and you're saying that they don't even have to meet their maker.'
'That's exactly what I'm saying,' she said, 'and those you think have no consciences are simply people that other people have mistreated. So don't be blaming God for a lack of judgment.'
It crossed my mind that this woman seemed to know exactly what was going on in this place, and yet I didn't know who she was.
'Who are you?' I asked.

'Just a woman advisor,' she replied.
'And your name?' I enquired.
'Lovely,' she said.
'Well, Lovely, how do you know all this?' I asked. 'Are you close to God?'
'I'm an advisor, I told you,' she said. 'I advise people of what they need to find eternal happiness in paradise. Do you understand?'
'I do,' I replied. 'But how do you know so much yourself? Did God take you under his wing, or are you living out some kind of purgatory?'
'Neither,' she replied. 'I'm doing this out of the goodness of my heart to answer your last question, and I learned of these things through experience to answer your first question. Are you satisfied now, the man who asks all sorts of questions?'
I smiled. I had been a bit premature. There were bound to be good people swarming around heaven – even if this "airport" was where we got the flight to heaven – and Lovely was only attempting to explain that to me.
'I think I understand,' I said, 'but I'm wondering why you do it.'
'To help,' she replied curtly.
'I'm wondering how God judges people,' I said. 'Is it by their looks, or by what's in their heart, or by what's in their mind? I mean I'm not great into revenge but the guy who killed me – or at least I think he killed me – seems to have got away scot-free.'
Lovely smiled again. She was really lovely and her name really suited her. She took a deep breath and tried to sum up the situation.
'We all know the circumstances up here,' she said. 'I mean all of us who've asked, that is. Some of us never ask. They just go by what God says. But I've asked.'
'Why did you ask?' I asked.
'I asked 'cos I was murdered,' Lovely replied. 'I was raped, beaten and left for dead and I died. So I was murdered.'

'Jesus,' I yelped. 'That's serious. But how do you know?'

'I was told eventually,' she answered. 'But that's not important now. In fact it doesn't matter at all since I know how human beings work, and I know that God has punished the men who did it.'

'How were they punished?' I inquired.

'They died,' she explained.

'No,' I said. 'You said people were "self-judging entities" and you and I both know that rapists do not just die. They go on to rape and kill others before they're caught. So how did they die?'

'They died in their souls,' Lovely replied. 'You know that you cannot get here unless you have a soul – and everyone is born with a soul and so everyone has got a chance to be in paradise. But their chance disappeared when they committed that grievous sin against me.'

'Is that all?' I wondered. 'Was there nothing more to it than that they lost their souls? Sure that means that they could have carried on doing their terrible deeds against other women. Did God really make us that imperfect?'

'No,' Lovely said. 'Death of the soul means many things happen. The sourness and the dourness of some people record the fact that they have little in the way of life. They are being punished for the deeds of their ancestors, and the sin can go on indefinitely until God intervenes.'

'So death of the soul can mean that they lose life and emulate death.' As I attempted to summarise her explanation, Lovely moved over a little and went to the aid of another passenger. I was lost again, but at least I knew something about what I was to face. I wasn't going to meet God. He had already judged me and found me worthy to have a chance at paradise.

That was an internal thing. I had come here of my own free will and in doing so I had basically been accepting God's judgment. I could still go to hell however and there were bound to be those who wanted to recruit people for that destination.

I looked around me to see if there were any little devils attempting to recruit me to go to hell.

A man approached eventually.

'Anyone looking to go to Mars?' he asked sincerely. I was impressed by his sincerity, and just for a moment, I thought that Mars might be where heaven was.

'Is that a trip to heaven?' I wondered.

'Whatever!' he said, again sincerely, but with a caustic tone mixed in.

'I want to go to heaven,' I said to him. 'I need to know.'

'Of course, it's a trip to heaven,' he said, less sincerely, and even more caustically. 'It just depends what your heaven is. God does not like to disappoint, so everyone goes to heaven, you understand.'

'Everyone?' I wondered. 'Jesus, how could that be? I mean - that devalues the efforts of those who have made an effort to get into heaven.'

'Yes, I know,' he said caustically, with a cruel tone coming through, 'but God doesn't like to disappoint, like I said.' He smiled then. It was a hollow smile as if he couldn't give a shit about anyone. 'Here,' he said, 'take a look at this DVD I've made of Mars to see if it is to your liking.'

I took the DVD and went into to a shop beside us where a sign said that DVDs could be played. It was a modern shop with all the latest electronic equipment, and I thought that I would soon learn something important.

I was no fool so I thought that I would learn that Mars was where God sent all the bad people to be punished. There was just something unpleasant about the man who had given me the video. His hollow smile and his cruel tone made me think that he was a little devil trying to recruit people to his paradise.

When I watched the DVD, I found out that I was right, but not in the way that I imagined. The human perception of hell was wrong. People were not roasting in flames with a devil fumbling around with a hot poker.

The dead seemed to be comfortable in their new abode. But it really was hell so far as I was concerned. They were living in hotels not homes, where all their food was brought to them and the place was like a palace.

How could they call this hell, I wondered at first. It seemed like a paradise. Certainly it would be paradise for some. But there was something missing.

Then I thought I noticed it. No-one was allowed to talk to anyone else. No, that wasn't it. No-one wanted to talk to anyone else. That was it.

It was another part of God's self-judging entity. The people chose to be in hell, but it was a hell of their own making. They didn't need to be unhappy, but if they continued on this road then they would become very unhappy. But they had chosen their hell, and they were in effect suffering even if they didn't know it.

The DVD kept stressing that they could leave at any time, and go to any other place, should they have wanted to, even if - it said – they were unlikely to want to leave.

I thought that if you were cut out for that place then you were cut out for hell. I was pretty sure that I was right as the DVD played, but I became certain when it got to the advanced stages of the advertising promotion.

I saw no children or old people on the DVD at that stage as it covered the latter stages of each week there. That was the orgy. It seemed like a fine orgy at first but the devil was making his way around all the women and impregnating them, it seemed. I didn't really know what was going on but I knew enough to know that this was not my kind of heaven.

I tried to understand what was missing and what I found was missing was feelings. These people had no feelings for each other. There was also a coldness in the facial expressions of the people there. It was as if they were doing what they were doing without the slightest bit of love in their hearts.

There were no rhythmic motions in the movement of their bodies. They were just doing what they were doing for the sake of it. I could detect a kind of coldness, a perverse, profound and scary coldness in the way that they had sex together. It was a real turn-off to me and yet it was meant to be a real turn on. In fact it was meant to be the final nail in my coffin as I made the decision to go to "Mars". It was unique selling point of this particular DVD and a great importance seemed to have been placed on the orgy.

It was hell on earth so far as I was concerned. I would prefer to see people with love in their hearts and goodness on their minds rather than see them escaping into this pornographic nightmare where everyone seemed about to become a victim of the devil.

I left the store and made my way to the main thoroughfare of the "airport" again. The man was waiting to hear my comments.

'Did you like it?' he asked abruptly from behind a billboard.

I looked around to make sure it was him and then threw the DVD at him. 'No.'

'I didn't think you were in the market for this trip,' he said. 'You're just not one of mine.'

I was still in shock at what I'd seen on the video. 'The trip stinks,' I said. 'What are you? Some kind of animal?'

'Fuck you,' he said.

I walked away then, letting the man get on with recruiting those who wanted to go with him to "Mars".

To my amazement a gate appeared suddenly in the "airport" that stated "Ireland". I decided that I wanted to give this gate a try. It had all the hallmarks of a genuine offer, and there didn't seem to be any glossy advertising or marketing push. It just seemed like the right thing to do.

There were people walking through the gate. They seemed like normal people, not sex-crazed perverts with no hearts as I'd seen on the "Mars" video. They had warm smiles and they looked as if they cared about the other passengers. They were offering to let the others go first, and when we eventually got to the "airbus" – which was a longish walk from the terminal – they were ensuring that the older passengers got seats.

At least they seemed to be older. Everyone seemed to look alike after a while in this place. I wandered over to the "airbus" and took my seat with the others. I couldn't help feeling that I was now with the decent people. I lay back in my seat – a very comfortable but not expensive one - and, after a few moments considering what I'd been through, I fell asleep.

I was on my way to Ireland.

Chapter Four

It was late in the evening when we arrived in "Ireland". It seemed like we had come a long way, and that the journey from the "terminal" of the "airport" had been a punishing one. I, like most people on the flight, had slept through most of it.

At the Ireland "terminal" of the journey we were feted with beautiful melodic music, music that was fit for kings, and the smell of a tasty Irish stew hummed in the background.

We didn't eat, however. We just smelled the food. It seemed that that was the way things were. We were not supposed to eat. I was not hungry in any case. I was simply enthralled at the prospect of getting back to my home country.

I looked around to see if I recognised the village we had arrived at, but I didn't see any identifying landmarks. I thought that I recognised the "airport" as Horan International Airport in Knock, county Mayo, near the shrine to Our Lady, but when I took a closer look it seemed that I had been mistaken.

It was more likely to be a little landing strip near a village in some remote part of the country where they were not aware that the angels were around.

We were taken to a bar in the nearby village where there was a session of traditional music going on. I liked traditional music, and the *craic* that surrounded it, but I was hoping that I might get back to my own city that night. I wanted to see familiar faces again.

Yet the faces in the bar all seemed familiar and it seemed that people rose to give us seats as we entered. I couldn't be sure since no-one seemed to leave as we entered and there were no seats left as we came in, so I wasn't sure how exactly we fitted into the place.

There were about twenty of us in all, all seemingly a little afraid of what they were letting themselves into. We weren't completely sure that we had chosen the right destination, and we were worried that we might be stuck with the devil for the remainder of our lives.

Although I knew from the video that you could leave the "Mars" orgy destination when you wanted, or at least that is what it said, I could not be sure that we could just get up from the Ireland destination and travel back to the "terminal".

At least the music was good in the little bar on the edge of the village. That was comforting. It was strange too since I would have normally needed a couple of pints of beer to warm to the violins and the accordion.

Then some of the locals began to sing along with the musicians. Or rather the musicians began to play tunes that they could sing along to. I was enthralled. Some of the songs were in English, so I could readily understand them. My Irish was not good when I died so I didn't really follow all the singing.

But my heart was burning for Ireland. I loved the country as I had always loved it. Yet this love was mixed in with feelings of longing. I longed to be back in the country as a full citizen and not as a ghost. Yet I didn't feel like a ghost. I felt like a soul, but not a ghost.

However, as the night progressed, I came to realise that it had been a long time since I had enjoyed a night like it. It was thoroughly enjoyable, the music blaring away, and creating tremors in my soul.

I met new friends too.

There was Jim from Buncrana in county Donegal, not far from Derry, who was getting drunk on the music and felt that it was "masturbating his soul". He kept having orgasms of the soul throughout the night and he seemed very happy. He kept telling me that he was never going to go home now. He wanted to stay in this village forever and a day.

But I still longed for home. I longed to see my mother and father, and my brothers and sister. I longed to see my uncles and aunts and cousins and to enjoy the craic with them. But mostly I just wanted to tell them that I was okay and that I was in heaven with these good people. For I knew that I had arrived in heaven.

I didn't want my folks to be worrying about me. I had died young and they were bound to be very upset that a young life had been cut short by whatever had killed me. I would have liked to tell them that I had arrived in paradise and I might one day see them there.

In any case the night was long and it was the wee small hours before we left the public house to go back to wherever we were staying.

As it turned out, we were staying in a communal house on the edge of the village. It was very large, just like an old-style mansion, and it looked positively frightening from the outside. It was the kind of place you would associate with Count Dracula in Transylvania.

Yet when we entered, it was absolutely beautiful. The living-room walls were covered in little drawings of what seemed like the children of the local primary school. There was so much love in the drawings that I shed a tear for the first time since leaving the "terminal". In fact, it was the first time I had cried since I had died, as I was too busy working out what was what at the "terminal" to think of crying.

Then I looked around me in the room and saw that the seats and tables were designed for little children, and I realised that I was actually in the main room of a school.

'Surely we're not staying in some school,' I said to my friend Jim.

'Jesus, I hope not,' Jim said. 'The noise will kill me in the morning with my hangover.'

'But you haven't been drinking,' I said.

'Sometimes the music gets you so "drunk" that you do have a hangover,' Jim said placidly.

'How the fuck do you know?' I wondered.

'I've been on the Ireland trip before,' he replied. It was a curious admission since he was admitting that he had left the

Ireland destination before too. 'We don't always stay in schools, but when we do, the children are really noisy in the mornings.'

'So you left here?' I asked. 'Why did you do that? I could never see me leaving now.'

Jim scratched his head, probably deciding if he should tell me the whole story. 'I went to "Mars",' he admitted. 'I spent my entire time there throwing up.'

'What about the orgy?' I asked, smiling like a child.

'That's why I went,' he admitted, very honestly.

'Did you go to it?' I asked, half excited, half disgusted.

'It was awful,' Jim said, his head lowered in embarrassment. 'It was absolutely fucking disgusting and it sickened me to the core. I kept throwing up, as I said.'

'Why was it so bad?' I wondered.

'It looks great from a distance,' he said, 'but when you're there you can smell the dirty whores with their sexual diseases, and hear their roars of pain when penetrated. You can see the dark red blotches on the men and you just know that they are dirty.'

'So they're all diseased?' I enquired.

'Yes,' he said, lowering his head again as if to emphasise the point. 'Never again,' he said, 'will I arrange another flight out of Ireland.'

I looked at him. He was absolutely shattered, whatever he'd been through. 'Do you think you've been to hell?' I wondered.

'Oh, yes,' he said, 'I've been to hell and back, and I really enjoyed being in that pub tonight. I am determined never to leave Ireland again.'

I was stupefied. He'd been to hell. How did he get in? I didn't need to ask how he got out since he was decent man. But how did he get in? I asked him eventually.

'You have a choice to make while you're in this place,' he said. 'You're a self-judging entity – as they call it - and you'll arrive at the destination you choose. You must decide what happiness is, and when you know, you'll know that God had guided you to paradise.'

'Happiness is what we had tonight,' I said.

'You're right,' he said. 'I was very happy tonight, and I've always been happy in Ireland.'

Ireland is truly a beautiful place. It was a real wonder that people would to leave it to go elsewhere. But there must have been temptations, I thought. Jim had succumbed to the temptation to find heaven in a place where sexual promiscuity was rife.

I nearly vomited at the thought of the smells he had described. It must have been a truly awful place. I was glad that I didn't take the man at the "terminal" up on his offer of a "flight" to "Mars". But I had known that it seemed to be like hell. I wondered about Jim. I mean - he must have known that it was an empty place where there was no love between people.

Some people believed the brochures about places, it seemed, and yet it also seemed that Jim had weakness for sexual relations. Despite that, Jim had chosen heaven.

I had a lot to learn, Jim told me when I explained my theories to him. He laughed off the suggestion that he did not know that he was going to hell. He knew that "Mars" was hell but he thought that he would give it a try just to see what it was like for those who had not made it to the Promised Land. He admitted that he had a sneaking suspicion that they were treated well and that they were happy down there.

'They were happy,' he said, 'to a limited extent. But they didn't seem to know any better. They didn't seem to know what true happiness was.'

There was much more to this life than met the eye, and I was determined to find out more in the next few days. We fell asleep eventually.

Chapter Five

The screams of children awakened me early in the morning. It must have been time for school so it was not that early, but I was still tired.

The screams became unbearable after a while and so I got up and went for a walk around the classroom. The children were chatting away about this and that as I circled them without them seeming to notice me.

'Look what I got,' Zoe said, as she took out a banana sandwich from her schoolbag.

'Mine's egg and onion,' Maire said, as she opened her sandwich and showed it to Zoe. 'Mammy said it is very good for you.'

I knew their names from their little name badges on their chests. They were innocent little children with strong west of Ireland accents. I couldn't determine what part of the west of Ireland they were from, but I heard one of them mention that they were from county Clare.

The teacher entered shortly afterwards, and all the noise died down. The children were taught to sit with their index fingers over their mouths to prevent them from speaking. Once in a while the teacher would have to roar that there was too much noise, and all would go silent again for a few minutes.

It was beautiful standing there at the back of the classroom, observing the little children as they learned their words and did their sums. They learned about Jesus first as they said their prayers and talked about God.

I had the strangest of impressions that it was meant to be me who was learning most when the little children learned. I was being treated to a refresher course in primary school knowledge and I was glad of it. The main thing that I was learning was that the children were so innocent at that age and nothing or no-one should ever attempt to take that innocence away from them.

The school was where they went to escape the pressure of home life, and the children made the most of it as if they would never get the chance again.

Of course, it was drummed into them that they would never get the chance again. The teacher would occasionally say to the little children that their parents never got the opportunity to go to school in such a new, modern school.

'Your school was an old mansion before it was renovated and made perfect for you,' the teacher would say as if the little children would know what she meant. But apparently their furniture was all new and the whole building had been reconstituted so that it was looking very well indeed.

I recalled that Jesus had said that, "In my father's house are many rooms." Perhaps this was what he meant. A little school with so many rooms and where so many little children learned about Jesus and about life.

Jesus said he would go ahead to prepare a place for us in his father's mansion. I smiled at the very thought of this little school with all the innocent little children, and my heart warmed at the thought of this being where Jesus had envisaged those who went to heaven would stay.

It was lunchtime when Aideen approached me. She had been on the "flight" down from the "terminal" the night before, and she had fully enjoyed the craic in the pub after our trip. She told me that she had shed tears for the children in her room. They had wakened her abruptly in the morning, but she was so happy to see them that she had sat listening to their every word during the course of the morning.

She felt that she had been given the task of watching over the children. It warmed her heart to think that God had given her that job. No-one had asked her, she told me, and she said that she didn't need to be asked. She thought that that was how God intended it to be. She had volunteered to do God's work, and she felt that this was how God wanted it to be.

'I'd love to think you were right,' I said. 'I would volunteer too. The children are just so good, and it's such a pleasant experience to be with them here.'

'But you don't think that is the intention?' Aideen asked.

'No,' I said. 'We have too much to learn.'

'About what?' she wondered.

'About death,' I replied.

Aideen laughed. 'We have to learn about death while these little children are learning about life. It's so unfair.'

'Unfair on us, or the children?' I wondered.

'How do you mean?' she asked.

'I mean that we've got the best lives of all now,' I said, 'and the children have to go through that awful period of exams, and spots and girlfriends and boyfriends.'

'And the period in your marriage when the love dies,' Aideen added.

'I never got that far,' I said.

'I'm sorry to hear that,' she said. 'Did you die young?'

'Twenty-four,' I said. 'Too young.'

'I'll shed a tear for you too,' Aideen said.

In the afternoon all of our group gathered in the grounds of the school, and went for a walk. I was very happy with this as I liked to see where exactly we were.

We walked into a forest just on the edge of the school grounds and, when we came to a clearing, we stopped and sat down on the rugged remains of some trees that had died and fallen over. We began to talk at that point.

'You all seem to be doing very well,' our guide said. His name was Thomas and he seemed to delight in what he was doing.

'Some of you might wonder why I'm with you at all,' he said. 'Are you wondering?' he asked.

'Yeah,' I said. 'I thought that there was no work in heaven.'

'There isn't,' he said. 'But I'm in purgatory. I'm doing my purgatory by cooperating with God in showing you the ropes. I'm hoping to be there with you in heaven one day.'

'I find that sad,' Aideen said. 'I mean it's lousy on you.'

'No,' Thomas said. 'I committed some very bad sins back there on earth, and really without God's guidance I would never have been able to identify where heaven was.

'Of course, my heaven is in my own country, Poland, and God does not allow you to become too familiar with your own country until you're ready to go there.'

'That really is sad,' I said.

'Yeah.' Three or four others agreed with me.

'How come we got here?' Derek asked innocently, as if he really didn't know.

'You're all given choices,' Thomas explained. 'When you exercise those choices carefully and you find that you've arrived in a personal heaven, then you really have arrived in a personal heaven. As you'll come to understand – because it will be said very often – human beings are self-judging entities.'

'What does that mean?' Derek asked.

Thomas smiled. He had obviously heard this question before. 'It means that you choose your own heaven. You're life on earth will determine what you will see as good or as evil. In other words, if you see good in hating human beings, even if you never actually say those words – for it is what's in your heart that matters – then you'll see good in one of the choices available. Only it won't be heaven.'

'And if you're basically a good person,' Derek wondered, 'you'll get to heaven?'

'It all comes out in the wash,' Thomas explained. 'And I mean that sincerely with all the profundity that I can muster. If you're a bad person at heart, you simply will spend your eternity searching for paradise. But even if you're here, and experiencing it, you may never actually realise it.'

'That must apply to me,' Kevin said. Kevin was a portly big man with a love of the smell of cigar smoke. He had spent the previous night sitting near to the bar trying to whiff the smoke of a businessman there.

'I cannot possibly comment,' Thomas said. 'Only God judges. I just inform people.'

'I didn't think last night was heaven,' Kevin said. 'And as for those bloody kids this morning, I couldn't wait to get out of the place.'

'Maybe you should take the next "flight" back,' Thomas said.

'Are you casting me out of "heaven"?' Kevin asked. 'You know I was a solicitor in a previous life, and I know all about the law.'

'It won't serve you very well up here,' Thomas said. 'The law of God applies up here, not the flawed laws of men. What made you great on earth may not even make you a little person up here.'

'Well,' said Kevin, 'I don't think that great people sit around all day observing children at school. Maybe you're all paedophiles, I don't know.'

There was a collective gasp from the rest of us there. 'I'm no paedophile,' Jim said. 'You're sick to take that from our watching over those infants this morning.'

'Yeah,' I said, 'we were watching over those children, not trying to take advantage of them. We're in our own personal heaven and dirty minds like yours should be sent somewhere to be cleansed.'

Kevin was stunned. The big baby broke down in tears, as if we had taken his dignity from him. He deserved all the condemnation he got for questioning the motives of those who had just journeyed to their "Irish" heaven. All they wanted was to be happy. The last thing they wanted was some cynic questioning their morality and their motivation.

'I want to go home,' Kevin said. 'It was alright there. At least I was with my family.'

'You should have thought about that when you drove at ninety miles per hour through a forty mile zone and crashed your car into the back of a crane,' Thomas said. 'What kind of person are you?'

'I'm a good person,' Kevin cried. 'I liked to help people.'

'I know,' Thomas said. 'You helped lots of people, but you've got to stop blubbering. If your life on earth wasn't a preparation for heaven then you'll have to go to purgatory to prepare yourself. That is, if there have been no complaints about you. If there have been complaints, the angels won't allow you into purgatory until you've seen hell for a while. They'll just want you to know what it's like in that awful place. It doesn't mean that you'll be there forever…'

'Stop this,' Aideen shouted. 'You're scaring me. Surely what this man does is his own business, and who or what he sees is his own business.'

'Sorry,' Thomas said, 'I got carried away there. I was just thinking of my own situation a few years back and I wanted to give Kevin the benefit of my own experience.'

'When you talk of hell, it's frightening,' I said, 'Some of us have just died and we're not really sure how we arrived in heaven so quickly.'

'I'll explain again,' Thomas said. He took a deep breath and continued: 'You're here because you're comfortable here. You like being here. You're drawn to being here. You've spent you're lives in such a way that you prepared yourself for being comfortable with an Irish heaven. I'll give you a profile of those who find themselves here: you'll tend to be Irish, with a strong conscience, with love in your heart for your fellow men, women and children, and with goodness in your nature. Does anyone still not understand that?'

'But isn't everyone like that deep down?' Derek asked naively.

Thomas laughed. 'No, not everyone is like that. That's why God created the universe in the way that he did. He gives us choices and – relatively speaking - we have free will to do as we please. He gives us an opportunity to prepare for the afterlife – broadly speaking that is – and we are supposed to do our best with our lives. Some of us prepare ourselves for hell, and some of us prepare ourselves to know heaven. Many of us end up in purgatory where we have to do some work in order to find heaven.'

There was a moment of silence then as everyone contemplated what Thomas was saying.

It occurred to me that Thomas had seemed to know how Kevin died, and so I wanted to know what he knew about my death. I strolled over to him after a while, wondering if I would ask my question if I was truly happy in heaven. As I opened my mouth I thought that I really didn't need to know now, and that I couldn't care less if Casey was brought to book for my death.

Thomas looked at me. 'You're wondering about your death, aren't you?'

'How did you know?' I asked.

'That's part of my training in purgatory,' he said. 'I'm taught to be sensitive to other people's thoughts and fears. What do you need to know?'

'You tell me,' I replied. 'I'm really kind of over the urge to know after arriving in this Irish heaven.'

'Well, you'd like to know how it happened?' he asked.

'No,' I said. 'Not anymore. But if the need arises again, I'll let you know.'

'Oh,' he said. 'You're entitled to know how you died and how your death affected the world you left behind.'

'Am I?' I enquired. 'Okay. Go ahead then.'

'I'm told,' he said, 'that you died as a result of a poisoning in the hospital. You were given an overdose of medication, and everyone thought you had died of natural causes. The pathologist covered up the cause of your death because he was part of a group hostile to you.'

I didn't need to ask what organisation the pathologist was from. It was the Knights of Columbanus. They had killed me, and I knew it.

I wasn't angry when Thomas told me. On the contrary I was full of pity for those who had taken my life. They would face the wrath of God one day. They would wander from heavenly kingdom to heavenly kingdom for an eternity trying to find their heaven and, even when they got there, they wouldn't know how to fit in. They would be uncomfortable for an eternity because they had killed me and because they had prepared themselves for an eternity of hell.

'You alright?' Aideen asked, as I walked away from Thomas in a pensive mood. 'You seem to have got a shock.'

'I'm alright,' I replied. 'I'm just sad that others were responsible for my death and that as a consequence they will go to hell for an eternity.'

'Oh, I didn't realise they can tell you. How did you die?' she wondered.

'I was murdered,' I responded with a tear streaming down my face.

Aideen came over and hugged me. 'There, there,' she said. 'I know I would be so angry to hear that if I didn't know.'

'I'm not angry,' I said. 'I'm bewildered about why they did it. There just seemed no need. It's so sad that heaven will be blocked to them now that they have offended God.'

Everything fell silent after that. I was gobsmacked when I had time to think about my death. I was really sad. It was a terrible thought that some people could conspire against you and cause your death as if you were some animal in the zoo.

Aideen shed a tear for me too when she heard how I was ill in hospital at the time of my murder and these people had drugged me and given me an overdose so that I had died in my sleep, unable to tell anyone that I was in danger.

I didn't even know that I was in danger, I thought to myself. I had believed that my illness would allow me some respite from my enemies, but it had not. It had only encouraged them to see me as vulnerable and, when they had the opportunity, they poisoned me. It was horrendous.

Nevertheless, what could I have expected from them? They were a bunch of cowards in life when I knew them, and that was not going to change just because I was acutely ill in a psychiatric hospital.

I sighed and Aideen sighed with me. She knew that I'd been thinking about my murder. She hugged me again.

'Don't worry,' she urged me. 'They may have won in life, but they will certainly not win in eternity.'

'Yeah,' I smiled. 'They'll spend their eternity up at the orgy being buggered by the little man with the hot poker.'

Aideen laughed. 'Or they'll be burnt to a cinder in the sun of "Mars". We both laughed at that. There was no escaping the verdict of the heavens. My enemies would never find the time to spend in a real heaven.

'If you're still talking about heaven,' Thomas interjected, 'you'll find that your enemies will have been complained about. Someone will have made a complaint. The angels watch the world very carefully and they know what's going on. When they make a complaint, it can be very nasty for those who have been complained about. They might go to hell for a very long time.'

Everyone looked at everyone else. Big Kevin was still there and was still awaiting his transfer to pastures new, where he thought that he had a better chance of finding his heaven. Everyone else seemed reasonably happy. I was delirious.

Then Thomas asked us all to get "into the mood" of things in heaven. He said that we could learn how to travel as fast as the wind if we wanted.

I was very keen, as were almost all of the participants. Even Kevin thought he would like to learn that. He must have thought that it might be necessary to know how to run like the wind wherever he was going.

Thomas taught us to jog first. It was easy since we were very light. But then, after about a half-mile, as we jogged across a field next to the forest, he shouted to us that we ought to get ready for a burst of wind.

Wheeeze! Whaaaaaooo! We were flying across the field like a greyhound, only faster. We were capable of high speeds. It was the greatest feeling that anyone could experience, I thought. It was like flying only our feet never really left the ground.

'This is heaven,' shouted Kevin. 'I think I might change my mind and stay with you.'

But when we stopped, Kevin had already rationalised that he could have learned how to run like the wind anywhere. 'No, I'm still going,' he said. 'I think heaven is somewhere else.'

'Wait until you learn how to fly like the birds,' Thomas said. 'You might change your mind then.' Everyone seemed to want to explain to Kevin that this was heaven, whatever he thought, and to urge him to stay. Everyone wanted him to be happy, but he was too thick about it. He seemed to think that he deserved to be in heaven, and that heaven should be shaped around what he thought it would be.

The rest of us were so glad that we were happy and content in this "Irish" heaven, and none of us really thought that we deserved to be there.

Chapter Six

Later in the evening, we learned how to run on water. It was fantastic fun. Thomas took us to a river and we ran along the bank at first. Then he shouted, 'You've got to trust me now,' as he moved slightly to his right and onto the surface of the river.

I ran so fast that my feet barely touched the water at all. Everyone was screaming and howling. It was the best laugh we had ever had. Heaven seemed just to get better and better. It was better than anyone had ever imagined.

Fish jumped over my feet as I moved rapidly down the river, and I was absolutely in awe of the experience. Aideen kept screaming that she was going to sink, but when I went to her assistance, she would laugh and race ahead of me. It was truly paradise, watching the birds stand on the branches of trees watching us, as we hurtled past them at perhaps a hundred miles an hour.

We sat down eventually at the source of the river where it branched out into a lake. No-one really fancied running over the lake as it was very wide and we could have lost Thomas or each other.

Thomas was well and truly knackered after teaching us about running and tiptoeing up the river. It had taken a lot out of him. The rest of us were tired too, but it seemed that a short rest would rejuvenate our energy levels.

I wanted to ask Thomas something else when I had time to get my thoughts gathered. It was about my death again, but this time I wanted to know why the angels, who were always looking over us, had not stopped the murderers having their wicked way with me.

'Why did they not prevent my killing?' I asked.

Thomas scratched his head. It was a question he had obviously heard before. But it seemed to be a tough question for him to answer.

'Do you know the answer?' I asked humbly. 'If you don't, it's alright.'

'No,' he said. 'The answer is that God allows things to happen. It would be unethical for God to intervene when the person who has died, or who is to die, will go straight to heaven. In other words, life is tough on earth, and it will always be more pleasurable to be in heaven.'

'But what if I was to go to purgatory, or hell?' I wondered. I was shocked that Thomas could be so matter-of-fact about my death.

'It depends,' Thomas said. 'The angels might allow for you to do some of your purgatory on earth by intervening and preventing your death. They might give you a disability instead, where the suffering would allow you to pay for some of your sins.

'If you were to go to hell when you died, and that was obvious to the angels, and it usually would be, then they would probably still allow you to die. There are no easy answers. Sometimes it suits the heavenly position to allow things simply to happen in order that they can reply to certain people's brutality or evil.'

'So God would have known that I was to go to heaven?' I wondered.

'Through the angels, yes,' Thomas replied.

'So what about this self-judging entity business,' I enquired. 'Surely God's angels are judging us, not just ourselves.'

'Yes,' Thomas said, 'you can think of it like that if you wish, but you must choose your destination on your own. It's your choice where you go. You're in heaven after all. You can, for example, go to the orgy in "Mars" just to see what it's like. The angels won't intervene to stop you. You are in the afterlife after all. But they know more or less everything about you, and they would be aware of where you will go.

'In other words, you have judged yourself to be compatible with the "Irish" heaven, just as the angels would have predicted, but they would never have attempted to persuade you to come here. Your previous life persuaded you that you were compatible with this heaven.'

'So I'm in charge of my own life,' I postulated. 'But there are those who would know all about my life. It's a bit of a contradiction.'

'Yes,' Thomas said, 'I suppose it is. But your self judgement is real in the afterlife, and your guardian angel is a reality in your earthly life.'

'I suppose,' I said. 'It ties in to what we think about our earthly life. But it's not what you expect when you get to heaven.'

'Why?' Thomas wondered. 'What did you expect?'

'Well,' I said. 'I expected to be judged by Jesus for a start.'

'Well you are in a sense,' Thomas said compassionately. 'I hope you're not disappointed. You are in a situation which you could never imagine, but it is not really all that different to what you expected. I'll tell you why.'

Thomas went on to explain that we were the chosen ones of God, people who had lived good lives and who were close to their soul. We had impressed God on earth and God had provided for us in heaven. He really had built the most complete enterprise in the history of the world.

People were judged, Thomas explained, under the self-judging entity mechanism because there were so many people and God could not spend all his time standing waiting for everyone to die in order to judge them.

'Was Jesus not to judge us?' I asked, not fully understanding the implications of Thomas' explanation.

'Jesus,' Thomas said, 'is the standard by which we are all judged. He is the way, the truth and the life. No-one goes to the father except through him.'

'What does that mean?' I enquired.

'It means,' he said, 'that Jesus effectively judges us by his standard. He isn't there, for the same reason as the father isn't there when you arrive in heaven –that is, because there are so many people involved – but he has set the standard by which you will go to the heights of heaven.'

'Is Jesus around?' I asked nervously, not knowing if my question was appropriate.

'Yes, Jesus is in heaven somewhere,' Thomas smiled. 'You'll probably meet him before long.'

I looked at Thomas. His reasoning was complex and his answers seemingly optimistic. But I believed that he was being straight with me.

I tried to summarise. 'So you're saying that God has set up a magnificent judging process that is seemingly so ultimate and intelligent – in the highest sense of that word - that on its own it takes care of the business of deciding who gets into heaven, and who does not.'

'More or less,' Thomas said.

'Yes,' I continued, 'and you're saying that God has set the standard for this process and its programmed into us so that if we are like Jesus – or if we try to be like Jesus – we will know heaven when we see it.'

'You'll be comfortable in heaven,' Thomas said. 'There would be no point in going to heaven if you think that its for wimps and sissies and those who are too soft. You wouldn't feel comfortable there, and so you'll take yourself off to wherever you want to go. Only it won't be heaven.'

'So,' I said, 'it's really the same thing as we believed on earth only God has a system all set up that determines that we self-judge and we find the heaven of our choice. Only sometimes it won't be heaven and we might not even know.' I thought for a moment. Something occurred to me. 'How do we know that this is really heaven?' I wondered.

Thomas smiled. 'That's the sixty-four thousand dollar question. You don't know until you've seen everywhere else. So do you really want to spend your eternity searching for heaven?'

'No,' I said. 'But where are the harps? There were meant to be harps in heaven.'

'We'll see some tonight,' Thomas assured me.

As soon as he said that, Thomas got up and beckoned everyone to take a good breath of "the fresh air of heaven" as we were going to somewhere special that night.

We took deep breaths and no sooner had we done so that Thomas had us jogging up the road towards a distant town. Soon we were moving like the wind again, past cars and lorries on the road as we travelled down the centre of it in a single file towards our destination.

On arrival there, we moved quickly to the centre of the town, to a place that Thomas had obviously been before, and we entered. It was the most magnificent theatre that I had ever seen. I wondered if we were really in Dublin and not some west of Ireland town.

Eventually we took our seats and the musicians came on to the stage. The music was beautiful, like it had been written by the angels themselves. I was absolutely in awe of this heaven yet again and I was wondering how it could possibly get any better.

True to form, just as Thomas had said, the harpists came on to the stage after a few songs, and they played their music with an elegance and a charm that I had never seen on earth. I was experiencing the full pleasure of the music now. It was getting right to my soul. I smiled as I thought that the soul was all I had now.

It was the most beautiful of nights, the most pleasurable I had had in a long time. Even the night before in the pub in the village had not been as pleasurable, I thought. There had been too much alcohol in the pub, blurring the enjoyment of the music to too many of the punters.

But this was heaven, I thought. This was greater than anything that you would imagine heaven would be like. We had Horslips music, Sinead O'Connor songs, melodies of The Corrs, and even the odd rendition of a Dubliners reel.

It was truly how heaven was meant to be. Rock music mixed into music of the soul. It was so exciting to be there. We were just commenting to each other how it couldn't get any better than this when another group would come on and the evening would step up to another level where the beautiful music and lyrics would be better than the previous group.

In one sense I couldn't wait for it to end so that I could sit up the entire night and talk about it with Aideen and my other friends. In another sense, I just wanted it to go on forever. But the pleasure was so great and the ecstasy of my soul so magnified that I knew one thing for certain: that it would end soon enough. So I really tried to enjoy it as much as I could while it lasted. It wasn't very hard to do that.

'You're forgiven not forgotten,' one song, from The Corrs, went. It was ecstasy personified. I could nearly hug the song, its spirit reached into mine and they made love like they had been waiting for each other all their lives. I practically felt like storming the stage when it finished and insisting that they played it again. But that wasn't the done thing.

Nonetheless, I was really getting into the music that night. Irish rock was my type of music when I was alive, and it was simply accentuated and made more beautiful while I was in heaven. It was the most beautiful of nights and I shall always remember it.

I went back to the school with a passion that night. We went to a different school this time, near to the town so that we weren't travelling so late. I was tired and I needed the sleep when we left the theatre, but a few deep breaths of fresh air and I was revitalised and keen to discuss what we'd been through with some of the other guests.

Thomas asked us to gather in a circle if we wanted to discuss the music earlier that night. He then went over to the corner of the room and put on a CD on the little music centre the teacher obviously kept for her students.

It was a CD of The Corrs. We were all delighted with the background music as we set about dissecting the night in the theatre.

Derek said the music was as good as he had heard in a long time, and that if some of those songs had been entered in the Eurovision Song Contest, they would have won it for Ireland without any doubt.

Kevin, who was still hanging around with our group, laughed at Derek's suggestion, and called him "an idiot" since they were all commercial songs and not Eurovision songs. Thomas immediately picked up on Kevin's criticism.

'You may have a point, Kevin,' Thomas said, 'but you must not go in for such sharp criticism of another heavenly body.'

Kevin laughed again. 'Heavenly body - that idiot.'

'No, Kevin,' Thomas said. 'There are no idiots in heaven. There should be no criticism but sometimes someone like you gets into the wrong place and the criticism flows. You know, that is part of your problem. You'll not enter heaven as an equal unless you give up that cutting criticism. It is said in heaven that "all criticism is self-criticism" and so you are really eating yourself up, and making it unpleasant for our new guests.'

'And what would you know,' Kevin roared, 'you half-assed, boot-licking, purgatory pixie.'

'Right, that's it,' Thomas insisted. 'You'll go to your room right now. You're simply not comfortable in heaven.'

I began to talk to Aideen at this and we talked of the night we had just had. Nothing was going to break the spell of our enjoyment of that night at the theatre in town.

'Heaven was never meant to be so good,' I said. 'I thought we'd be sitting around, listening to the angels playing classical music all day.'

'Yeah,' admitted Aideen, 'I thought we'd be sitting on feathered cushions and having grapes brought to us by the angels.'

'It's so much better than I thought too,' I said.

Aideen smiled a broad smile and breathed deeply the night air: 'It's so exciting. It's like being a child again, learning to do things and then doing them ourselves. I can remember teaching my children and my grandchildren all these things – walking and running.'

I contemplated her words for a moment. 'How old were you when you died, Aideen?' I wondered.

'Eighty-three,' Aideen replied. 'And yet I'm so young now.'

'You're eternally young now apparently,' I said. 'There's no ageing in heaven.'

'Who told you that?'

'I'm just guessing,' I said. 'You are just the same as me. You look just as young as me and yet you died three times as old as me. So there can't be any ageing in heaven.'

Aideen smiled. 'That's a beautiful thought.'

'No, I mean it,' I said. 'Everything is so beautiful that the God who made all this possible must have made our ages the same in heaven. It just sounds so right. I don't even need to ask.'

'I hope you're right,' Aideen said. 'And funnily enough, I think you've guessed just perfectly.'

We hugged each other, and there was love present, which made things seem even more beautiful. I was so deeply happy.

Chapter Seven

I wakened suddenly at eight o'clock in the morning with the sound of the caretaker unlocking the doors of the school gymnasium. We were still assembled in a circle, only all of us were lying on the ground attempting to sleep.

The caretaker kicked his leg against a chair as he carried a box towards the front of the room and he roared out of him: 'Ya hoor's ghost, ya.' He wasn't amused at all.

I laughed at the thought that there might be a whore's ghost in the room with us taking offence at him for his remark. I looked around me at the ghosts, or the souls, laid out on the ground, resting, to see if there was any reaction. But there didn't seem to be.

'No whore's ghosts here,' I said. I took a deep breath and I was becoming fully awake again. I took a few more deep breaths, noting that the others were beginning to do likewise at the various ends of the room. We were all stretching and absorbing the morning air as if it had been weeks since we last rose from the ground.

I cringed at the thought that we were ghosts now, but I was also realised that we were in paradise and that nothing could ever hurt us again. We were perfected in a way that we could never be on earth. The very thought of being afraid of a ghost was beyond me now. I could never fear the dead. I could only ever fear the living and what they could do to each other. In fact I was aware that so many bad things were going on in the world that it beggared belief that God didn't just shut the whole thing down.

Instead he had created a perfect system where we chose the surrounds that we were comfortable with, and so we chose if we were to go to heaven or not. It was strange too that the guardian angels would always know who would make it to heaven. That meant that there was an element of preordination, and that God must simply have known what kind of person to make to ensure that they got to heaven.

Then there was the genetic argument. I asked Thomas what he thought of the predetermination-by-genetics argument that some racists used on earth.

'It's all very much nonsensical in heaven,' Thomas explained. 'First of all genetics proposes that certain people are the best at certain things. They do those tasks well, and these tasks tend to be oriented towards the maximisation of wealth. Health is wealth on earth. Money decides many things on earth.

'However, the most genetically perfect people wouldn't necessarily be the most desirable in God's eyes. It's quite the contrary on almost all occasions. If people breed in order to advance their financial interests then their genes will be pretty good. But their soul might not be too healthy.

'If people avoid relationship with people with bad genes, even though their heart dictates otherwise, then they become shallow, and their soul will be damaged. They may end up with pretty good genes, but they may have absolutely no chance of getting to heaven.'

'I think I understand,' I said. Actually it was a pretty good explanation. It was pretty obvious to me that all those racists who stated that certain people were inferior on earth, or just plain imperfect, were likely to be very inferior themselves. It was just how Jesus had said it would be: that there would be those who would thrive on earth, but who would never know the "kingdom of God". "The first would be last, and the last would be first [in the kingdom that is to come]."

It made sense of course that Jesus would know about these things. He was after all the Son of God. But more than that he had been taught by the angels, and the lessons of the angels were what I was learning now. I felt so privileged.

The children arrived after a while for their morning classes. They were older children that day, and they seemed much less keen than the younger children who seemed to have taken everything at face value. These children were a little cynical, much more so than their younger colleagues had been the previous day. They were obviously at a stage where they were having to grow up, and this meant that they would see things much more through the eyes of a struggling teenager than through the eyes of a child.

Life was stressful for these young people. There was no doubt about that. They were at a time when their pubic hair was beginning to grow, and their bodies were generally on the change. Some of the young girls there had the beginnings of breasts.

The young boys were beginning to look handsome. Their features were beginning to change from their naturally beautiful childhood features, which were soft and tender. Some of them were beginning to look tough, and I didn't like that. These boys were on the wrong road, I thought.

The teacher was a kind old gentleman, whom they called "wee Tony". He would seek to punish them if they disturbed his class by taking them out to the hallway and pretending to slap them. He would bang his strap off the window shelf and urge that you "don't do it again.' He was very funny and all of us had a good laugh each time he took one of the students to the hallway.

When it was time for lunch, we took a deep breath and we inhaled the smell of the soup on offer in the canteen. It was a beautiful smell, and we were very contented. We were also full up, so we had plenty of energy to continue with our adventures with Thomas.

After lunch, Thomas took us to a clearing in the trees surrounding the school, and we sat down to listen to what he had to say.

'Talking,' he said, 'was one of the most important things that you do in heaven. God likes to hear you talking. He doesn't like you to hold things in. He likes you to be open and understanding of each other, and to communicate any concerns you may have to each other, especially those that involve other members of your team.'

'Are we really talking?' asked Lorraine, one of the quietest of the group.

'Yes, we are,' Thomas said. 'We are talking to each other in a very clear and distinct way. Do you not think so Lorraine?'

'Then why don't the pupils hear us?' Lorraine wondered.

'That's a good question, Lorraine,' Thomas said, scratching his head.

'Telepathy,' I shouted. 'We're talking in our heads and we're able to listen to each other's thoughts.'

'Good answer, John,' Thomas admitted. 'Yeah, I think that that's the truth. John's answer is as good as it gets. We're telepathic. We communicate through our heads and we don't make much in the way of sounds.'

'That must be how they hear the dead at the psychics' shows,' Lorraine said. 'I've been thinking about it, and - you know - they bring people to these shows on earth where the psychics tell them that their deceased relatives are trying to contact those in the audience. It would be nice to tell my relatives that I'm safely tucked away in heaven.'

'We could make arrangements to go to one of those shows tonight, if you all wish,' Thomas said. 'But it is a purgatory thing. It's not really done in heaven. Well, it's not really supposed to be done in heaven, and some of the guides are extremely strict about it, but we could take a sneaky trip to one of the shows.'

I smiled as I knew that one or two of my relatives would go to these shows from time to time, and they would probably be there tonight since it was shortly after my death. So I was hoping that Thomas would take us to a show near Derry. In fact, I found out that all of our group were people either from Derry city or Inishowen, the neighbouring area in county Donegal, so I was thinking that Thomas would take us back there for a night with our relatives.

'First,' Thomas said, 'you must learn how to fly.'

'What?' Aideen roared. 'How are we to do that? Isn't it enough that we can run as fast as the wind?'

'Everyone knows how to fly in heaven,' Thomas explained excitedly. 'It's the one of the greatest experiences of all.'

'I'd like to see this,' Kevin said under his breath. 'Some of those old dears have never been in an airplane, never mind flown of their own accord.'

'Don't be so bloody cynical,' I said to him. 'Those old dears are just as energetic as you now.'

'Aye!' Kevin said sarcastically.

'We must first summons a host,' Thomas said. 'Our host will carry us as far as we like within reason.'

'Some of you might even get as far as that school,' Kevin whispered.

'You just summons the flier by shouting "flier" in a high pitched tone,' Thomas explained. 'Then hopefully a flier will arrive.' He screeched "flier" then.

Suddenly there was a flock of birds over head, and as Thomas used a high-pitched tone to bring them to us, a series of bird shits landed on the ground beside us. We were laughing our heads off at this stage, and Thomas was feeling like a bit of a fool.

The birds landed on the grass beside us, and we stood staring at them, wondering how something so small could carry all of us. Thomas then explained that we would have a bird each to carry us up to the sky. It was still a bit dodgy to ask each of us to put our trust in one of these birds.

'Watch me,' Thomas said. 'These birds are magnificent. They can do almost anything.' Thomas ran toward one of the birds and entered him. He just seemed to disappear down the bird's throat.

'Let's go,' he shouted.

The bird flapped its wings and rose gently off the ground. It rose up into the sky and flew around in a circle for a few moments and then came gently down to earth again. It was absolutely frightening to us to think that we had to enter a bird. We wondered if the bird would eat us. But Thomas re-emerged from the bird, and told us everything was fine.

Aideen and I tried it next. We ran to two birds sitting on the ground and we dived into each of their mouths.

'How do we move?' I shouted to Thomas.

'Just tell it what to do?' Thomas said. It'll understand.

'Fly,' I said, and my bird immediately rose from the ground, its wings flapping heavily. It was the most tremendous experience that I had ever had in my life.

'Whaaaoo!' I shouted to Aideen who was just behind me.

'Brilliant,' Aideen said.

We looked down to see about fifteen birds coming after us.

Thomas was at the front of the birds. You could just see his head protruding from his gull. 'Let's tour the country,' he shouted.

We went south first to county Kerry, I believe, since there were so many lakes and some islands off the coast. We then went across to Cork and the city seemed to be very busy since the traffic was backed away along some roads beside the River Lee. In Dublin, we saw Phoenix Park where the residence of the president of Ireland and Cleopatra's needle were beautifully situated. We went north to Belfast, and saw the great cranes in the docks.

Then we went over Derry. The walls of the old city seemed much smaller in comparison to how I remembered them, but I recalled how we were seeing them from the air and that's just how they would look. The Foyle Bridge was magnificent and we flew under it, then twisted around and flew back to the top of the Foyleside Shopping Centre in the city centre, where we came to rest.

I was breathing air very deeply as we travelled so I wasn't tired at all. I kept telling Aideen to do the same since she was beside me almost all of the way, and she said that she was ready for more as soon as we arrived.

'We're beside the theatre now,' Thomas said. 'The show will be on soon. Take deep breaths and recover your energy.'

We took deep breaths as Thomas said, and on his instructions, we got the birds to land outside the doors of the theatre. There we came out of the birds and, as the birds went back to the top of the shopping centre next door, we gathered ourselves together and readied ourselves for the show.

The psychic was a strange enough looking man when he came on. I was glad that we were fairly near the back, and we weren't sitting too close to him, though he made us relax quite quickly, and he had the most pleasant of voices.

I could see none of my relatives when I looked around at the beginning of the show, but Aideen noticed two of her daughters in the seats near the front.

Thomas tested out the psychic very quickly into his routine and found that he was "quite good".

'He's quite easy to communicate with,' Thomas said, as he explained to Aideen what to do.

Aideen made her move soon after, totally uninhibited now that she was in heaven. She raced at the psychic and dived into his mouth, and tried to communicate with him.

'I can see two girls in the audience, maybe twins, no not twins, but very close,' the psychic said. 'They've lost an older relative, a woman, a much loved woman. Does anybody recognise any of these things?'

No-one came forward at first. The mention of the "girls" had put Aideen's two daughters off since they were both in their fifties. I shouted to Aideen that she should say that they're quite old now, and the psychic seemed to hear me.

'The girls are quite old now,' he said a few seconds later, 'but mammy remembers them much younger.'

Straight away Aideen's two daughters jumped up in their seats and screamed that they knew who it was. 'It's our mother.'

'Yes, well,' the psychic said, 'your mammy just wants to tell you that she is very happy where she is, and that she loves you both very much. She says don't worry so much about her, and say your prayers and bring your children up to love Jesus.'

'Where is she?' Jennifer, Aideen's youngest daughter, asked.

'She's in heaven,' the psychic said, 'and she's as happy as Larry. She says she had never had craic like it.'

Everyone laughed at this, but I was crying. It was just so beautiful to think that you could talk to your family from the afterlife.

'She wants one of you to get a new kitchen, and the other to get a new marital bed,' the psychic said. 'Does that mean anything to either of you?'

'I need a new kitchen,' Jennifer said. 'And my sister here has just got a new bed for her and her husband.'

Everyone gasped. It must have seemed like such a coincidence.

I looked around then and two women entered at the back of the theatre beside me. 'Jesus,' I gulped. It was my mother and my sister. I could hardly contain myself. But it was typical of them, always late.

What was I to do? I wondered. I could let things sit since I didn't want them to think that I had come to a psychic's show just to speak to them. They would be going to every show after that thinking that I would be there.

But the temptation just to say a few words that might give them comfort was too much, and I turned to Thomas and asked him for any tips.

He told me to try to situate myself as near to the psychic's brain as possible, and to speak as clearly as possible to him. But he was very clear about one thing: that we couldn't give exact details since that was not done in the spirit world and because it would give people certainties about heaven that they weren't ready for.

I raced forward as soon as Aideen had finished. I positioned myself right over the psychic's brain and I began to speak – very clearly.

'There are another two women in the audience,' the psychic said. 'They have lost a very valued member of their family recently. He's younger than one of you and older than the other. Does that make any sense to any of you?'

'It could be us,' a woman in her fifties, near the back, shouted. Mammy looked so very sad. I was determined to cheer her up.

'Your son wants to speak to you,' the psychic said.

There was a scream from my sister but my mother was silent and dignified. 'What is it he wants to say?' she asked.

'He wants to tell you that he is in heaven now,' the psychic said. 'He is very happy, and you shouldn't worry about him as he is with the angels and God.'

'Tell him we miss him very much,' my sister shouted.

'Tell him we love him very much,' my mother said.

'He loves you both very much,' the psychic, 'and he says that it is important that you get on with your lives now, and that he will be waiting at the gates of heaven to ensure that you get in. But he doesn't think that there'll be any trouble.'

I raced to hug my mother as soon as I had finished speaking. I could her speaking. 'That was our John alright. A wee joke thrown in at the end to ensure that we weren't worrying about him.'

'He's a wild man,' Marie said. 'Always has you shedding a tear.'

I tried to tell them that I loved them again, but there was no response. They simply didn't have the faculties of the psychic. But at least they knew it was me. I was so happy that I cried my way through the remainder of the show. I cried even through

Kevin's unseemly antics with an old woman, which caused a stir.

After the show, we flew back to a school in the west of Ireland, and so our education continued.

Chapter Eight

We were so excited that we sat up all night talking about our experiences with the psychic and our families. It was a very beautiful experience, and each of us looked forward to the day we could do it again.

Even the performance of Kevin didn't change that. Kevin had sat on an old woman in the audience and learned some things about her by reading their mind, a skill that he had learned in another part of heaven, probably purgatory.

When he had finished he had gone into the psychic and waited on his turn to grill the relative. He had asked the psychic if anyone had lost a loved one in the last few weeks, a person who loved his grated cheese.

'Here,' the old woman shouted. 'My husband loved grated cheese.'

'Did he play football with Derry City?' the psychic had asked.

'Yes,' she had shouted at the top of her voice. The woman next to her had begun to scream.

'Did he retire with a broken leg?' the psychic had asked.

'Yes,' the old woman had screamed, overcome with emotion.

And just as the woman was going into ecstasy, Kevin decided to play a dirty trick on her.

'He says that you should keep milking the goats?' the psychic had said. The woman had gone into despair at that, as she had no goats. She had begun to cry.

'It's not me,' she had wept.

'For a moment there, I thought you were on the right track,' the psychic had said. 'It's sometimes unfortunate that there are coincidences in heaven, and I suppose there are so many people on the other side that they can get mixed up at times.

Kevin's dirty trick had almost soured the whole night. It was a dastardly act and we all told him so at our new school that night.

'I don't give a shite what you think,' he had said. 'Do you think that you were much better down there boasting to your relatives that you got into heaven.'

'We weren't there to hurt anyone,' I had said. 'We were only trying to help them with their grief and their loss. I don't suppose anyone was grieving over the loss of you.'

'No,' he had thundered. 'But they'll miss my sense of humour.'

'I'll give you that,' I had said. 'It was funny, but that old woman will never live it down. It was also cruel, depraved and a very good reason for keeping you in purgatory.'

'Fuck off,' he had told me.

Thomas came over then and suggested that Kevin would be better getting on the first "airbus" back to the terminal, which would be in a few days time. He said that it was a long time since anyone had ever carried out such a cold trick on a member of the public at a psychic's meeting and he was so desperately embarrassed among his peers, some of whom were there that night.

He practically came to blows with Kevin and I think that the only thing that held him back was his own personal desire to work off his purgatory peacefully, and to be in heaven one day.

We talked endlessly for the remainder of the night about the encounters we had had with our relatives, about the warmth of the smiles on their faces, about the sincerity of their belief in the psychic's power, and about the sense of spirituality in the crowd at the event. It was a most beautiful night and I was so happy.

I had never known any set of experiences to be more enriching than these experiences. They were majestic and revolutionary. If I had known that heaven was so good while I was alive, I would have been the first in the queue to get there.

I looked back at my life at that point, and thought that it was so hard that it just could not compare to the excitement and the craic of heaven. All the exams that I had ever done had not prepared me for the completeness of the set of experiences I was now going through.

I was truly in heaven, not just in a metaphorical sense. I had always known of heaven as an abstract notion while I was on earth. We had said things like, "this is heaven" to describe a moment in time when we felt very contented. But I never really and truly thought that we'd ever see the day when things would be so complete and so beautiful that I would describe them as being everything that you would expect of heaven and more.

Nevertheless, we were at that point now. Nothing had ever been so perfect. Nothing could have ever been so good. It was the culmination of an adventure so profound and so outstanding that these words and a hundred more like them could not have adequately described the experience.

It was an experience of experiences. It was perfection amidst a desire to make every moment last. Nothing had ever been like it before.

We were on a learning adventure and we were becoming like angels in the sky. We were learning to be in heaven and yet heaven was earth with attachments so perfect that we simply could but make the most of it.

Next morning, which came quickly as we had hardly slept, I asked Thomas about Kevin's incursion into the old lady's head at the psychic night.

'How'd he do it?' I wondered. 'He seemed to be able to read her mind.'

'That's a skill that's hardly used,' Thomas explained. 'I'll teach you about it later today, only because Kevin's let the cat out of the bag; but it's a skill that should only really be used in very rare circumstances.'

'Is it part of the devil's knowledge?' I asked.

'No,' Thomas said. 'It's to do with certain sensitivities that have developed over the years since angels began to use that skill.'

'Are you teaching us to be angels?' I wondered. 'It seems we get more like them every day.'

'Goodness, no,' Thomas said, 'but I see where you're coming from. We're teaching you to be good members of the heavenly congregation. Some of the skills are the same, but angels have very great intelligences and they get involved in everyday life on earth. Do you really want to be an angel?'

'I've never thought about it,' I replied. 'But seeing some of their skills, I can see that there would naturally be an attraction to their way of life.'

Thomas went over to Derek then for a chat, and I could hear them mumbling away about this and that. Derek seemed sad at that moment. I could see no reason for it, but I heard his "mammy" referred to a few times. She mustn't have been in the audience that night.

The schoolchildren arrived that morning too, and I was delighted to see that we were in all-girl school. The girls were so much more responsible than any of the other children. They also seemed much more settled and even happy. But they had their work to do just like the other two classes.

It was a wonder how these children coped with all the work they had to do. I marvelled at the weight of their schoolbags and the length of some of their home-works. They had obviously to deal with their own hell on earth.

I was happy when we got out into the grounds of the school for our afternoon chat. We stood together on the edge of the school grounds and we were all smiling at the thoughts of the previous night.

Then Thomas began talking about telepathic communication with living beings.

Apparently it was only to be used very rarely, only when we were in difficulties or when we absolutely needed the information in the person's mind. There were no strict rules about it as such, but the conventions were very insistent: we had to be careful how we used the information we gathered inside someone's mind.

'Is it easy to do?' I wondered.

'It's pretty straightforward,' Thomas explained. 'But it's very tiring. It will take a lot out of you. If you do it for any length of time, you may be exhausted and unable to re-emerge from the mind until you regain your powers – which could be days away.'

'How is it done?' Michael, a Creggan man who had just passed away and was on his first visit to heaven, asked.

'You simply enter through the mouth and go straight to the brain,' Thomas explained again. 'You will then face a lot of information coming at you, and that is why it is so tiring, and you will have to wait several moments before you can begin an interactive communication with the person.'

'When that happens, you're in someone's conscience, and you'll hear a lot of personal stuff. You'll hear their innermost feelings, feelings that they may not even know about yet, and you'll get a lot of personal information passing through you.'

I was amazed at what Thomas was saying. It seemed that we had the power to dredge through people's innermost thoughts and feelings.

'That just doesn't seem ethical to me,' I said. 'We shouldn't be able to do that.'

'That's why it's to be used very infrequently,' Thomas said. 'The angels only ever read people's minds to find out if they are worthy of the Kingdom. The angels also keep a gentle eye on the affairs of families, countries and kingdoms to ensure that things are generally going in our direction.'

'So why tell us about it at all?' Michael said. 'It seems so unnecessary to anything we may ever need.'

'Oh,' Thomas said. 'You must know everything. You're in heaven now, and I hope to be with you eventually, so I know about it too. The only reason you're finding out about it so soon is because Kevin - our old friend over here who's returning home soon - effectively told you about it last night at the Millennium Forum theatre in Derry. So, you see, I had to be reasonable with you, and I had to ensure that you were not left wondering at what Kevin did. It is an easy enough skill to use, but it is something that you should really only learn from an angel himself or herself. You'll be meeting angels soon enough.'

We moved on to talk about other things after that. Thomas sat back a bit then and allowed the rest of us to exercise our "speaking" skills, which were in reality telepathic communication skills. It was a long afternoon, as everyone had a query about the psychics show the previous night.

'Did you talk to your mother?'

'Why were your brothers not there?'

'Where was your father?'

These were just some of the questions I was asked, and there were plenty more as the hours passed. I was genuinely tired at the end of it all and I wondered about the psychic's show: Was it really worth all the hassle? I understood why our guide wanted to play it down a little. But it *was* worth it just to see my mother's face and hear her words indicating that she thought my remark was a typical joke from John.

I was happy at that. It was beautiful and simple.

In the afternoon, we decided with Thomas' advice to relax things just a little. Thomas felt that we had fallen for the trap of taking the psychics show too seriously, and were becoming a little too anxious about what happened there. So he wanted us to go fishing.

But it was fishing with a difference. We hitched a ride with a flock of seagulls and made our way to the ocean. There we had to dive into the cold waters of what we were told was the Atlantic Ocean.

It was absolutely freezing for the first few moments that we were there, but once we got used to it, it warmed up ever so slightly and gradually until it was quite tolerable.

Then we went searching for a shoal of fish in order to do our fishing. Thomas recommended that we start with a shoal of smaller fish like mackerel so that we didn't do ourselves any damage. The bigger fish would come much later.

We found a shoal fairly quickly, and it seemed to be a shoal of cod. We took a deep breath at the surface of the ocean and dived deep below. We then entered the fish through their mouths, and inserted ourselves just beside their brains.

We could control them, just as Thomas explained, and we could ride with them for long periods, as we were not using very much air. It was the most exhilarating experience yet to see some of the most beautiful sights that the ocean bed had to offer. The colours of the fish and the coral at the bottom of the ocean were sights to behold. No-one had ever created anything so perfect since the beginning of the world. Nothing had ever been more inspiring than this natural piece of the Earth at the bottom of the Atlantic Ocean off the coast of little Ireland.

I could have stayed there forever if the air supply had have allowed it. But, as it was, we were under the water for the best part of an hour each time we went under, and we could control the fish to come to the surface if we needed to breathe. It was a truly wonderful thing to be able to do a tour of the ocean. I couldn't wait to get into the head of a whale or a shark.

But as it was it was the best adventure we had been on at that stage. At one point a shark passed near the shoal and made a dash right into the centre of our group. I wasn't worried about being eaten, as Thomas had told us that we should not panic in such circumstances since we could move through the shark, out its mouth and up to the surface.

But as the shark consumed some of the fish in our shoal, I could hear the screams of Aideen as she struggled to get out of the fish inside the shark. I made to rescue her by instructing my fish to swim right up to the shark and force it to eat us. When he did, I was in the shark's stomach along with Aideen.

'Calm down,' I shouted. 'Are you stuck?'

'Yes,' she shouted, 'I can't get free.'

The fish was clearly dead and had closed its mouth very tightly. I wedged open its mouth. 'Move now,' I told Aideen, and she moved quickly out of the dead fish's mouth and into my fish's mouth.

'No,' I said, not wanting her in my fish, which was dying. 'We have to get to the shark's brain.'

We swam to the shark's brain, and took refuge there. But we were both tired and almost out of breath. I tried to control the beast in order to get it to move to the surface, but it was resisting my urges.

Eventually, Thomas arrived over and moved in beside us in the shark's brain. He urged the shark very forcefully to go to the surface and we were safe again.

Aideen was delighted with her adventure, as I was. We thought that it was great, even if it had been a little dangerous. Nothing could compare to a real adventure and it made our experience of heaven even more meaningful.

That night we talked for a moment about what we wanted to do, and we all agreed, except for Kevin, that we'd like to have an adventure again. At first we didn't really know what kind of adventure we would like, but we eventually came to an agreement that we'd like to spend the night in what was described in our locality as a haunted house.

We called for some birds to take us there and, when they arrived, we set off for McArthur's farm on the outskirts of a neighbouring village. It was very dark when we arrived there, and since Thomas was winding us up a fair bit, we were all a little scared of what we would find. Except for Kevin, that is, who thought that it was all a load of old balderdash.

We entered the building through an open upstairs window, but we could hear the farmer himself sitting downstairs watching television. He was living there on his own since his wife died, and he was a very old gentleman who still did a bit of farming to keep himself active. But he was semi-retired and looking for the sweet life.

We set off to discover if it was a real ghost who had been playing up and causing concern for the locals, or if it was just a figment of their imagination. Thomas was no help this time. He suggested that we'd have to learn about this ourselves. Of course, he told us that we had nothing to fear, but he said it in such a way as to imply that we would really have something to fear when we encountered the source of the rumour about the ghost.

I was a little afraid that we might meet a devilish ghoul who would attempt to scare the wits out of us. But we tiptoed around the house, going from one room to another in order to find this ghost. Eventually we decided that he had to be hiding in the attic.

So we let off screeches that would have literally wakened the dead, and hoped that only the ghost would hear the telepathically-transmitted sounds. It wasn't long before we found out.

There was a screech back from the attic, and we ran like mad to hide under the covers on the beds. We were so scared that it was a long while before we moved from the beds, and tried to communicate with the ghost.

'Who are you?' Thomas asked.

'Mrs McArthur,' the ghost replied.

'What do you want?' Thomas asked.

'Peace,' Mrs McArthur said.

'What do you mean?' Thomas asked.

'I'm not a happy dead person,' Mrs McArthur said.

'You're not?' Thomas wondered.

'No,' she said, 'I'm in purgatory.'

'There are happier ways of doing your purgatory,' Thomas suggested.

'How?'

'Like teaching the people from heaven,' Thomas advised.

'They're all wankers,' Mrs McArthur said.

'Wankers?' Thomas asked. 'That's a bit strong.'

I thought I knew what was going on. 'Kevin? Is that you, Kevin?' I shouted.

'You found me out, you bastards,' Kevin shouted. 'I'm only trying to wind you up.'

'Good wind up, Kevin,' Thomas said cheerfully. 'You had me fooled, but obviously not everybody.'

Then we heard this scream downstairs and Mr McArthur came running to get his shotgun. 'Don't come near me, you mad bastard,' he shouted.

'Kevin!' Thomas shouted. 'You know that that's not right.'

Kevin came out, laughing his head off. He had moved right down through the house and appeared to Mr McArthur. It seemed that we were in line to have a new skill taught to us during the next lesson: creating an apparition.

It took several whiskeys to calm Mr McArthur, who must have put it down to the family ghost again.

Chapter Nine

After a good night's sleep, we woke to find ourselves in one of the bedrooms at Mr McArthur's farmhouse. We had sat there talking for much of the night. The craic had been good, and so we had decided to remain until the morning.

In the morning, we could hear Mr McArthur on the telephone telling one of his relatives that he had heard the banshees all night and that he had seen for himself the ghost at the farm for the first time. He said he was going to get the priest to exorcise his home as soon as he could come, and he was sure that either he, or someone close to him, was going to die soon because that was what the presence of the banshees meant.

I wondered about the noise of the banshees. I thought that it might have been Kevin up to his old tricks. But Kevin was adamant that he had not done anything that would have merited the description the farmer gave of the banshees. I had not heard anything myself, so I decided to investigate.

I was looking all round the house when I came to the farmer's bedroom. I could see the bedclothes hanging off the bed, and in the corner of the room, I could see something that I recognised immediately. It was another "ghost".

'Who are you?' I wondered.

'I'm just a passing soul, who's spent many a year here in this old house,' came the reply. His voice was trembling, whoever he was.

'Why are you afraid?' I asked concernedly.

'You're terrorising me,' the voice replied. 'I've been shaking and screaming all night. The old man has heard me for the first time, and he thinks that I'm a banshee.'

I laughed heartily.

'What are you laughing at?' the ghost asked.

'We're supposed to be afraid of you,' I explained, 'and last night we were petrified of finding you.'

'The feeling was mutual,' the ghost retorted. 'I don't think I was ever as afraid in my entire time on earth.'

I laughed again. He was a sad, pathetic sight hiding in the corner of the room like a trapped mouse, but he was the most remarkable of ghosts. He was afraid of other ghosts, as if they could do him some harm. I smiled at the very thought of a ghost being afraid of ghosts, but I recalled that I had been in that situation myself the previous night.

The old ghost laughed too. 'I suppose it's a bit silly, a ghost being afraid of ghosts. But I heard one of you scare the old man and it really sent me into a panic.'

'I understand,' I said. 'That was Kevin. He's doing his purgatory at the moment and he's acting like a spoiled boy.'

I promised the old ghost that we'd leave him alone as soon as we'd dealt with the old farmer, who was still waiting on the parish priest to come.

When the priest came, Thomas had advised us what to do.

In the middle of the priest's prayers, we began to make the room vibrate a little, causing the lamp stand to fall over, and sending several glasses in his wall cupboard flying.

The priest was trembling as this happened, but we stopped as soon as his prayers finished, and there was silence. Thomas felt that this would indicate to the priest that the exorcism had worked and that the ghoul had left for a different place. It was hilarious to us, but we supposed that these were the things that we had to do in order to restore peace to the old man's home.

It was a most amusing moment to see the old man smile again and think that his home was free from spirits.

I couldn't wait until we learned about these apparitions. It was an enthralling prospect to think that we could create a vision for someone else to see.

It wasn't long before Thomas took us to a clearing in the forest near old Mr McArthur's farm, and we were instructed on apparitions.

Thomas wasn't at all comfortable with these apparitions, but by popular demand he acceded to our requests for a full explanation of how they were actually done. He said that they were rarely undertaken, and that they should only be done with the best of intentions.

He told us that Kevin would be answerable for his apparition the previous night, and it was fortunate that they had limited the damage he had done by creating the illusion of tremors so that the farmer could feel that he was at peace with the spirit world now.

He told us that apparitions were mainly used in the religious and medical domains. There had been many religious apparitions, he said, and there was a ready-made audience that was willing to believe everything that they were told about these apparitions and their message.

God had sincerely sent messages to the world through these religious apparitions and it was a favourite form of communication for Him. They were usually simple messages, but sometimes the messages were profound or symbolic.

It was a beautiful way to pass a message since it often involved people who had illnesses of the mind. These people were consequently more valued in their communities, and it reinforced the meaning of God's use of these people, which was that these people were human beings too. We were all one family, the entire human race, and we were one under God, the children of the one true God.

In medicine, people had apparitions all the time. People who suffered from such diseases of the mind as schizophrenia and manic-depression often received auditory and visual hallucinations during their episodes of illness.

These people were sometimes the vehicles that God used to get his messages across. God had a purpose for these people,

Thomas said, and in the afterlife they were among the most able of the congregations. Some became angels since they were so powerful, and when they rose to that level, they were often the favourites of God.

But, Thomas explained, an apparition was essentially a hallucination, but it was controlled to such an extent that it became very real to the person concerned. Even if that person had never suffered from a debilitating illness, it was still likely that most people would assume that they were "crackers" at first. That meant that the message, if there was to be one, had to be very carefully thought out to ensure that it made sense to someone with an expert level of wisdom, like a priest.

Sometimes there was no message and the real purpose of the apparition was to encourage people to get involved in the worship of iconic things like the Virgin Mary. The apparitions of Mary were the most beautiful ones that God engaged in, and were a personal favourite of God Himself, and they inspired people to seek real beauty and true love in women.

In order to perform a hallucination, Thomas told us that we had to enter the subject's head and move straight away to the linkages between their brain and their eyeballs. There, they would find a mechanism for overriding their subject's visual abilities. Intense concentration would create images in the vision of the subject, and a hallucination would be created.

But it took great concentration and very intense thoughts to ensure that a meaningful hallucination was brought forth. Thomas was agitated as he spoke. I sensed that he really didn't want to reveal this kind of information.

'You're not happy telling us?' I asked him.

'No,' he said, 'it's not that. It's right that you should know, but it is a bit soon to know about one of the great skills of the afterlife.'

As a form of light relief from the study of hallucinations, Thomas told us that the angels were sometimes very cunning in what they wanted people to believe. For example, the angels didn't like some Americans, and the American capitalist system didn't appeal to them at all.

So the angels like to play with the lack of belief in God that certain Americans, and also certain Europeans, had. One thing that signalled a lack of belief in God was the belief that UFO's inhabited outer space and were abducting people and generally flying over America, doing as they liked.

I smiled as soon as I heard Michael mention the UFO's. It was one thing that I wanted to ask him. I wondered how there could possibly be UFO's while God had all this technology at his disposal. There was of course only natural technology in God's hands but it was extremely powerful, and the thought that aliens could possibly threaten mankind was fanciful.

'It's a paranoid complex,' Thomas explained, 'to believe that aliens in UFO's are more powerful than God. It's totally irrational, and yet the myth has grown in recent decades in line with increasing technology. We're beginning to get afraid of ourselves in philosophical terms, I think.

'But it's particularly pertinent in the United States, and the angels encourage it by creating hallucinations and hallucinatory journey's in order to persuade people that there is such a threat.

'It's hard to know why they're doing that. They just don't seem to like certain attitudes in the advanced world, which largely depend on the absence of any sort of God, and I think they want to punish them by making them seem discredited when the truth gets out.

'"You believed in UFO's, you fool," sort of thing. They would look so silly if God could prove to them that his angels were encouraging these hallucinatory experiences. It's a bit harsh on them, but then they're being a bit hard on God now.'

'It's hilarious,' I interjected. 'There are millions of Americans out there, building armaments dumps and telling the whole world that the aliens are coming. On the back of those primal fears, Hollywood has made movies about aliens, and alien abductions, and alien attacks on New York and the USA as a whole. It's absolutely hilarious!'

'Yeah,' Aideen said. 'It means that America, for all its faith in God, and I know that there is a lot of that faith, partially believes that there is no God to protect them and that they're the ones who have to be ready when the big monsters come to eat them up.'

Everyone laughed.

'The angels are worse than me,' Kevin said. 'I mean I only got the old farmer to see a ghost because I wanted to make everyone laugh. It backfired to an extent because he ran looking for a shotgun, and got a priest to bless the house, but the angels are deliberately winding up the Americans and making them believe that they really are under threat.'

'But the angels do everything for extremely serious reasons,' Thomas said. 'They wouldn't do it for a laugh. They are doing it to expose the lack of belief of these Americans, and indeed some Europeans, who've become a little distant from God.'

It was indeed a very funny topic when I thought of it, but as Thomas had explained, it was also very serious.

Thomas then took us to a herd of cattle in one of Mr McArthur's fields, and we practised hallucinations.

It was the funniest thing that we had done to that date. The hallucinations really scared the cattle, but Thomas said that was preferable to scaring human beings. And he was right.

We got up to the most awful tricks with each of our cows. They scampered here and there across the field and back again. I had to warn Thomas that one or two of the cows was showing signs that they were exhausted, and I was fearful that they would take a heart attack or rupture themselves.

Kevin, of course, was up to his old tricks. He got one bull in a corner of the field to see a "beautiful" cow, and when it went to mount the cow, it found that it had landed on a wall. It nearly burst its bollocks, and roared for several minutes in agony.

Kevin was truly a bastard.

I took Kevin aside after that and had a chat with him.

'What's wrong?' I asked. 'Why are you pulling all these strokes?'

He was much miffed by my questions. It seemed to me that he was attempting to impress the heavenly congregation, and he thought that we were responding. But some of the things he was doing were not that funny.

'In any case,' I told him, 'we're not really impressed by people who use other people for their humour. You may think that we enjoy your pranks, but we don't when we have time to think of the reality of what you have done.

'We're pretty straight people, us heavenly dwellers, as Thomas sometimes calls us, but we do have a sense of humour. We like what you do on the surface, and we laugh and enjoy your pranks somewhat, but we don't get the idea that you have to use somebody who's at a disadvantage to you to get your point across.'

'That's what humour's all about on earth,' Kevin argued.

'No,' I said. 'You're wrong. That's what sometimes is wrong with humour on earth. It depends on hitting out at people who don't have the ability to defend themselves. It uses people, and yet the funniest thing is that one day the very same people who are using other people for their humour are at the bottom of the heap and the joke is on them.'

'How?' he wondered.

'Well,' I replied. 'The joke is on you now that you're in purgatory and we are in heaven.'

'But I'm able to stay here if I want,' Kevin argued.

'Yes,' I said, 'but you're a self-judging entity, just like us, and in the end you'll decide to live out your purgatory with other purgatory dwellers because you're not really comfortable with being with us. Isn't that the way you really feel already? Isn't that why you're playing all these pranks? Isn't it just a way of getting our attention and making yourself feel less alienated from us? Isn't that right?'

'I suppose,' Kevin said. 'But it must be no fun living in heaven. You're all too straight, and your sense of humour is different to mine. I'd rather be in purgatory if it means I can avoid living like you lot in this place.'

'Purgatory,' I told him, 'was no different to living in this place. But one of the pleasures of heaven was that we could see all things as they really were, and we had to understand when people or even animals were abused that it was contrary to the will of God. You'll never get out of purgatory unless you learn that lesson.'

Kevin was very upset in reality. He knew what I was saying, but he lacked the maturity and the sense of responsibility to agree with me. He didn't like to see anyone getting one up on him. He didn't like anyone telling him the difference between right and wrong. He didn't like the idea of anyone knowing more about the world than him. To me, it was a question of values, and his middleclass upbringing had not given him the kind of values that would make him entirely comfortable with heaven and its sense of the essential equality of people. It was inevitable that he would spend some time in purgatory.

Chapter Ten

I thought that our conversation would serve to tame Kevin, but I realised that we would soon find out whether he had really changed at all. We were going to a hypnotist's show that evening, courtesy of Thomas.

I wasn't sure it was a good idea after all the practise at making hallucinations we had with the cows on Mr McArthur's farm earlier in the day, but Thomas felt that we had to see a hypnotists show in order to witness some of the angels in action.

It was to be the culmination of our introduction to heaven. It was to be one of the greatest experiences we were to witness, and Thomas said it would inspire us for years to come.

We were intrigued by what he had to say. Nothing, surely, we felt, could equal some of the experiences we had to date. Nothing could be more beautiful than "fishing" inside fish or flying inside birds. Nothing could be more perfect than creating a hallucination so that a dumb animal could get excited and out of breath.

I marvelled at this experience of heaven, and thought that, though it was an "Irish" heaven, it could so easily have been in any part of the world. We were fortunate to have found our very own palace in an experiential sense, and we were happy to be as near to God as possible, again in an experiential sense.

This must be what is meant by being in heaven with God, I thought. I asked Aideen what she thought of it all, and she told me that the experiential heaven must be a practical solution to the problem of having so many millions of people living in heaven.

'God couldn't be seated among us all,' Aideen explained.

'I think you're right,' I told her. 'Of course, we would all like to see God one day, just to be sure that we're in his good books.

But if he was to spend his time meeting dead people, he would never get a minute's peace.'

We were all looking forward to seeing the angels in action, so we went with relish to the hypnotist's show. We sat at the back of the ground floor of the theatre where there were some free seats, and we listened to the hypnotist begin his show.

He talked of relaxation and suggestion, and he gained control of his audience pretty quickly.

Soon there were people up on the stage, and the hypnotist seemed to have them in a relaxation-based trance, just like ones I had seen many times before while on earth.

Then he had them doing all sorts of tricks, and the audience were eating out of the palms of his hands. He was a very able hypnotist, like one of the top quality hypnotists I had seen before on earth. He had the people up to all sorts of things.

There were a few risqué moments during the show as it progressed, and I was delighted just to be in the audience and not on stage.

Eventually I began to wonder what Thomas had been going on about. There didn't seem to be anything too special going on. Then I focussed on the fact that he had mentioned angels and, after a few minutes thinking, I felt that I had it cracked. The angels were making a complete ass of the hypnotist.

The hypnotist was the last person who would realise it but he was being made to look like a complete fool. The angels were doing all the tricks. It was they who were instructing people to act like idiots and make all sorts of ridiculous efforts at things.

At first sight the hypnotist looked ever so clever and competent. He seemed to know everything about his job, and about how to relax people. But he could not know what was involved when someone chose to come up on stage. That was to do with the angels.

Nevertheless the hypnotist was good. He *was* clever and professional. But he was dealing in magic powers, powers that could so easily be abused. So the angels were stepping in to ensure that he was kept on the straight and narrow to the greatest extent possible.

I concluded that they were inside the people on stage, were switching off the volunteer's consciousnesses and taking over. It was as simple as that. It was the perfect moment. I felt utterly satisfied that I was right. It was beautiful.

I laughed and I laughed. The others began to wonder about me as they could not figure out what was so funny about what was going on up on stage.

'It's the angels,' I shouted, and they looked at the stage again. They didn't see them, but I could. What was going on the stage was just a little more than perfection. I laughed some more, and eventually the others began to catch on. Thomas and I began to explain to them that the angels were inside the people on stage, and they were making it seem even funnier than it really was.

Soon everyone in our group was falling around laughing at the antics of the angels on stage. There was a little twist of a bum here, or a thrust of hips there, that were carried out in such an amusing manner that it could only have been the angels. The reactions were simply too sharp for humans to undertake.

Aideen was in stitches at this. She was so chuffed at being able to see the angels in action that she was in ecstasy. She was having an orgasm at the back of the theatre. Soon I was too, and all of us had had orgasms within a few minutes of each other.

The angels loved the hypnotist's show. They loved performing, and they loved the warmth of the audience. I could sense their enthusiasm from the back of the theatre, and I knew that they really were in their very own heaven.

But they were really good. No-one in the audience, apart from us, had any idea that they were there. The hypnotist had absolutely no idea that they were taking the piss out of him and making the show seem even more funny.

At one point, the hypnotist told a member of the audience to sing like Elvis. Everybody knows Elvis, having seen him on stage or in the films, but which Elvis did the hypnotist want?

Did he want the young Elvis or the older, fatter Elvis? The only person who seemed to know with any certainty was the man requested to sing like Elvis.

He stomped onto the stage and began to sing and swivel his hips at the same time. He was pretty good at it, and I could sense fairly quickly that the angels were encouraging him to do his own thing. He was just too good to be acting on his own initiative.

He jumped all over the stage and I knew that it was the angels giving him the energy to do as he pleased. He was like a young child all over again, and he was alive.

That was what made the efforts of the angels so perfect: the people were alive. They were living out a potential that could never be theirs in any other circumstances. They were in a kind of relaxation-induced heaven and the angels were having some fun at their expense.

But it was responsible fun. I could detect that. It was fun with a purpose, like the fun associated with giving some American citizens the fear that aliens were coming to get them. The angels were probably trying to tell us something about our culture, where we like to laugh at the few while we were seated among with the many.

They were probably saying that the joke was on all of us there since none of us really knew what was going on at the show, and we were all being fooled. Even the hypnotist was being fooled, and the biggest joke of all was on him. The angels were telling him not to try to out-angel the angels, not to try to make himself seem so clever at the expense of others, since it was they who invented such powers and not him.

When it came to the hallucinations I thought that I was pretty accurate in my estimation of what the angels were up to. This was sacred power and the angels were ensuring that they kept control of it.

Some people thought that they could see a cinema screen at the back of the theatre, where they sat sadly and happily, angrily and enthusiastically, through the screening of a non-existent film.

Then the hypnotist gathered them for the party piece of the evening: to see him as an invisible man.

'This is going to be something,' I told Aideen. She nodded her head, and smiled in anticipation.

'It's going to be marvellous,' she said in reply.

It was marvellous at the very beginning as the stage volunteers began to run screaming from the hypnotist. The audience were in raptures as the hypnotist carried the microphone stand across the stage and the stage volunteers ran like scared children to get away from him. Of course, they couldn't see him and they thought that a ghost was carrying the microphone.

It was marvellous craic, absolutely brilliant. But I knew that only the angels could carry off such a trick, and that the hypnotist himself was being conned into believing that he had those powers. He had no such powers, despite being absolutely full of himself, thinking he was the bee's knee.

I thought that the hypnotist was absolutely hilarious. He was as vain as anyone could possibly be, and yet he was striding around the stage as if he owned the theatre. No, it was much more vain than that. He thought he was God Almighty. I laughed at the very thought, but it was almost unbearable to see him traverse the stage and make all these volunteers seem like fools.

Then I looked and I couldn't believe what I was seeing. Aideen and some of the others were getting up on the stage and attempting to get involved in the show. It wasn't the done thing, but I thought it might be a good idea and, at the time, I came to the conclusion that it was. So I jumped onto the stage myself.

I got inside one of the volunteers and there was an angel in there. He was very powerful, fully able to throw me out again, but instead he told me to relax and enjoy myself. It was a stunning sight to behold. I could see the hypnotist's microphone stand wandering around the stage, but I couldn't see the hypnotist himself. The angel was controlling the volunteer's viewing.

The angels then decided among themselves to scare the wits out of the hypnotist. One of the volunteers went near him and came out of his volunteer like a big ghoul. The hypnotist moved back, but he wasn't that scared, as he had seen things like that happen from time to time.

Then I could see an almighty rush of angels towards the microphone stand. Something was wrong, I thought instinctually. Suddenly the microphone was being wrenched out of the hypnotist's hands and a volunteer pulled it back, and levered it over his body.

In fact, it hit him straight over the head, and he fell like a sack of spuds to the ground. No-one seemed to know what had happened, but the angels quickly took control of the microphone through another volunteer and the show went on temporarily without the hypnotist.

'Who's that blaggard?' the angel in my volunteer asked me.

I looked over and I could see Kevin. He had obviously taken our chat badly, and was playing up again.

'It's Kevin,' I told the angel. 'He's a purgatory man, but he's been hanging around with us.'

'The bastard,' the angel said. 'He needs a kick in the backside. He could have ruined this show, and he might have killed the hypnotist. Is he out of his mind?'

'He's a bit of a spoiled boy,' I said. 'He gets up to everything.'

'A prankster?' the angel wondered. 'Well, I know what to do with a prankster.'

Everything got back on an even keel again soon afterwards. The hypnotist got up and continued with his show. The audience settled down again, and the volunteers continued to do funny things.

I didn't know where Kevin had gone, but we were all happy as we got up to leave. Then there was an almighty kafuffle near us at the back of the theatre. I thought it was one of the volunteers doing what the hypnotist had said he would do after the show was over. I had seen this before at hypnotism shows and it usually involved volunteers running off to find their Easter bunny or such like. But this one seemed much more anxious.

'Let me out, you bastard,' the volunteer was shouting. He kept shouting and I was very keen to find out what was going on. So I went inside the volunteer.

'He won't let me out, the bastard,' Kevin was saying as he fought vigorously against this very powerful angel inside the volunteer, the same volunteer who had slammed the microphone stand over the hypnotist's head.

'What's wrong, Kevin?' I asked humorously. 'Do you not like being on the other side of a prank? Do you not like someone not treating you seriously?'

'The fucker,' the volunteer shouted. 'He has me trapped.'

'Who?' asked the hypnotist who had just arrived over, wondering what had gone wrong with his simple suggestion.

'The arch-angel,' the volunteer roared in reply.

'Relax,' the hypnotist told the volunteer. 'I'll get rid of the arch-angel.' The hypnotist, who was totally perplexed, thought he would try something and so he then addressed the arch-angel: 'Leave him alone, arch-angel.'

There was an almighty roar out of the volunteer, and he reached his right leg back and swung it right between the legs of the hypnotist.

'Jeeeeesuuus!' the hypnotist roared. He fell to the ground for the second time that night, and rolled around on the ground like a wounded pig. He was mortified. Never before had so many things gone wrong in one of his shows. Never before had he been so embarrassed by the pranks in his show.

'I'm going to give this lark up,' he groaned. 'I'm losing my touch.'

'Let me out, you maniac,' Kevin roared from inside the volunteer. 'You'll have me in jail for something I didn't do. It wasn't me. It was the arch-angel.'

'He's fuckin' possessed,' someone shouted perceptively.

'I'm his brother,' a man said. 'He shouldn't have been up on stage. He has an illness, if you know what I mean. He only wanted a bit of craic.'

Then the volunteer pulled back his right arm and landed a very solid punch on his brother's chin. His brother immediately fell to the ground and began to groan.

'Let's get him to a doctor,' a man said.

'It was only a punch,' someone said. 'He'll be alright.'

'No,' the man said again. 'I'm a psychiatric nurse. This boy needs restraining. He's obviously ill.'

The last we heard was that, when the doctor interviewed Kevin's volunteer, he had given him all of Kevin's details, and so Kevin was admitted to a psychiatric hospital for the first time. He was not a happy camper.

Eventually, after the doctors got his real details from his brother, and they found out that the real Kevin had actually passed away months before, some of the doctors began to think that he was possessed on the night itself. But the volunteer would recover after a few weeks of treatment and would be released quickly back into the community.

The angel explained to us that he had been the sacrificial lamb for the things that had gone wrong on the night of the show. Somebody had to be to blame or the game would have been given away.

Kevin's dilemma caused great amusement among our group for days after. The angel explained that it was his own vanity that would make the experience in hospital extremely burdensome for Kevin, and it was a trait of most people in purgatory and a few in heaven to be afraid of these situations. There was nothing to fear, the angel said, in psychiatric hospitals. They were a place of refuge for people who had become ill, and most were out before they knew it.

We couldn't help but smile when we thought of Kevin being held captive in a place where he would only find discomfort.

'The poor soul,' Aideen smiled.
'Aye,' I said. 'He's probably in a padded cell by now.'
Everyone burst out laughing at this.

Chapter Eleven

The next day we went down to the local psychiatric hospital, Gransha, to visit Kevin. We were genuinely concerned about him because he was such a silly man that he was bound to be doing something to upset the applecart.

When we got there, we went through an open window and into the ward. We could hear Kevin's screams from a distance so we knew that he was somewhere in the building. We searched for a while and found him lying in a bed inside the hypnotist's volunteer he had turned into a maniac the night before.

The volunteer had been given special leave to lie on in bed because he was doped to such an extent. There was a nurse sitting near the volunteer, watching over him.

'Kevin,' I whispered. 'Are you still in there?'

'Yes,' Kevin shouted. 'The bastard has cast a spell on me and I can't get out.'

I smiled and there were a few giggles from behind me in the queue of heaven dwellers.

'What do you mean - he's cast a spell on you?' I wondered.

'He's a bully,' Kevin replied. 'He's a big powerful angel and a bully, and he's taking it out on me.'

'I'm sure this gentleman you're inside would have a few words about you being a bully if he knew what had really happened last night,' I told him.

'I was only carrying on,' Kevin said.

'What about the big bull?' I reminded him. 'He wouldn't think that you were just carrying on. He was practically castrated.'

'It was intended as a joke,' Kevin said. 'Just like when the shark swam into the middle of your shoal.'

'You did that too!' I shrieked.

'Yeah.'

'Well, I don't feel so bad about you being here after all,' I told him. 'Do you know that Aideen was very anxious inside that shark? And all because of your prank, you son-of-a-bitch.'

'Forgive me,' Kevin said. 'I was a fool.'

You were more than a fool, I'm afraid,' I told him. 'You were a danger to our way of life.'

'I was only playing,' Kevin argued. 'I like playing. I like to please people.'

'You like to please the wrong people,' I said. 'That's what the problem is. You're a delinquent and a fraud.'

'No,' Kevin cried, the tears visible from where I stood looking over him. 'I'm a good boy. I would never hurt anyone deliberately.'

'Okay,' I said, 'but you'll have to serve your time in this volunteer. We're not powerful enough to break an angel's spell. You'll have to see what it's like when life goes wrong and when your health fails. I think that's what the angel had in mind. Even if he didn't have it in mind, I think it's a good idea for you to see people suffering. Is that okay?'

'Okay,' Kevin said. 'Now go away.'

'We'll go when we're ready to go,' I roared.

'Get lost.'

Just for his insolence we decided to go downstairs onto the ward and wait for Kevin. There we encountered a whole plethora of patients with various illnesses. They all seemed to be trapped inside their bodies.

One of our group had been here before as a patient during the course of his life, and so he could explain what was going on. We decided that we would prepare a little surprise for Kevin when he appeared inside the volunteer.

We all took our places inside each one of the trapped patients, and awaited Kevin's return. Aideen thought that we should all try to emulate Jimmy, one of the trapped patients, who had a habit, we noted, of exposing himself to other members of the household. She thought that we should all expose ourselves to Kevin. But I advised her that we should only do that with Jimmy since the nurses were watching.

Kevin arrived soon enough, and we began by introducing ourselves to him.

'I'm Billy.'

'I'm Mickey Joe,' one patient said.

'I'm Charlie,' another said.

'I'm Jimmy,' yet another said. It was really the heaven dwellers inside the men, but Kevin felt that all the patients could talk to him. We had reinstated their cognitive abilities just for a few minutes in order that Kevin had the impression that they could communicate with him.

We knew that we had to take advantage of the fact that Jimmy pulled out his penis in order to impress Kevin.

Eventually, when everyone had said "hello", we got Jimmy to pull out his penis and approach Kevin's volunteer.

'What the fuck?' the volunteer roared when he saw that Jimmy was standing beside him with his penis sticking out.

'He does that sometimes,' one of the nurses told him.

'Does what?' Kevin asked in trepidation through the volunteer. Then he looked down and saw that the patient next to him was holding his penis in his hand and trying to rub up against him.

'Aaaaagh!' he roared through the volunteer. 'Get me out of here!'

'It's alright!' the nurse shouted. 'He's just saying that he likes you.'

'I like you too,' Charlie shouted at the other side of Kevin. Kevin looked around and Charlie was playing with his flies.

'Jesus Christ!' Kevin shouted. 'They're all queer in here.' He looked earnestly at Charlie and said: 'I'm not ho-mo-sex-u-al. Do-you-understand? I am not ho-mo-sex-u-al at all.'

Mickey Joe looked at Kevin when he caught his the eye and shouted: 'We're not ho-mo-sex-u-al either.'

Kevin looked at him and saw that he was scratching his bollocks. 'What are you then if you're not queer?'

'We're just frustrated men,' Billy said, as he stood there, with his hand slipped down his trousers.

'I hope you don't think you'll be taking out your frustrations on me,' Kevin warned him. 'I'm not that kind of person.'

'None of us were that kind of person when we first came in here,' Mickey Joe said. 'But this is what time here does to you.'

'How long have you been here?' Kevin asked.

'Thirty-one years,' Mickey Joe said.

'Whaaaaat? And they haven't let you out?'

'What's wrong, Kevin?' asked the nurse, who could only hear Kevin speaking.

'This man has been here thirty-one years,' he said, 'and no-one's seen fit to let him out. There's nothing wrong with him. He's just a queer who likes the sex in here.'

'I'll have none of that,' the nurse said. 'These patients are all sick and they know nothing about sex.'

Kevin looked over at the four patients who were winding him up. All of them rubbed their groins and smiled at him.

'I'm fucking going now,' Kevin said agitatedly. He ran at the nurse, and hit him an almighty blow to the side of the face. Another nurse, who had been observing the situation, caught Kevin by the arm and pulled him back until his colleague had recovered his composure. Then they restrained Kevin.

'You are only here for a few days,' the first nurse said by way of calming Kevin. 'The only reason you were sent to this chronic ward was that you were violent on the night of your admission. Your sedation is wearing off and we need to sedate you again.'

'These patients are all queer,' Kevin roared.

'How do you know?' the nurse asked. 'Do you know that none of these patients has talked to anyone in twenty years?'

By now Kevin was getting the message. He looked around and, because he couldn't leave his own "volunteer", he shouted telepathically at us: 'You bastards, you had me going there! Now get lost!'

We fell about laughing as we left Kevin to his own devices.

I never had craic like the craic I was having now. I had been to university in Galway but the craic there was different, even if it was also extremely enjoyable. We were like children again when it came to fun, but our powers were so advanced that it was like being God. We could do almost anything. In fact, there were few things that I could think of that we could not do. A whole new world had opened up to us.

Each day I went for an adventure with some of the others, or on my own. I was deliriously happy. I could barely help myself for fear that it would end and I would be back in the hospital again, feeling all the feelings of despair and hopelessness.

I could not countenance a world without the powers and skills that I had now. It would be a meaningless world, and yet it hadn't been that long since I had none of these powers, and I was only a mere mortal on earth.

If only people knew, I thought. If only people knew that getting into heaven was not that hard and that the benefits of being there were absolutely massive. Yet how could the angels tell ordinary mortals that they would one day be gods if only they were good to others?

It was a difficult question and the answer had to be that we were not gods, just the inhabitants of heaven, and God was so much more powerful than us, and even the angels: He was all-powerful and we were still junior members of what was a massive source of power.

We were gloriously powerful and we had the power to make things better on earth. That was the thing that I noticed most. We had the power to influence events. We had the power to watch over people on earth, people in need or in difficulties. We had the power to make a difference to the lives of every single person on the planet and we were doing it.

There was no doubt that we were doing it. We were helping to make the world a better place.

So I decided that I would ask advice from Thomas, who was bidding us farewell to continue his studies for heaven with a new group.

'What's the chances that I could get away with sorting out the people who had killed me on earth?' I asked.

'It's not very wise,' Thomas said, 'but if you feel strongly enough you should probably talk to an angel. They'll usually understand why you need to do a thing like that.'

So I went to meet an angel.

Chapter Twelve

I searched for an angel all the following day. When we weren't looking for one, they would pop up everywhere. But when I searched for one, I could not find one anywhere.

I knew that they were quick and that they would only be seen when they wanted to be seen, but I thought that I would find one fairly easily since I was a heaven dweller.

I summonsed a bird and we flew over the countryside, looking for one of these elusive characters. But apparently it was not a good idea to try to find an angel from a bird's eye position.

We flew to a castle instead where I felt that we would find an angel, or if not, someone who knew where to find one of them. There were a few signs that the angels had been near the castle, as I could see cattle that had been disturbed below me. So I was hopeful when I entered the grounds of the old building.

It had been converted into a hotel, so the castle was quite plush and comfortable. I left the bird at the hotel gates, walked to the front entrance, and sat hopefully on the steps at the front door. It was so creepy I wondered if there were any ghouls around.

'Angel,' I shouted. 'Are there any angels inside?'

Suddenly there was a high-pitched scream at a window several floors above me, and a ghoul appeared.

'What do you want?' he asked loudly.

'An angel,' I said.

'Get lost,' the ghoul shouted.

'Where would I find an angel?' I asked, thinking that he might know.

'Get lost,' he shouted again, 'I don't know where the angels are now.'

'Where would they usually be?' I asked, noting the "now" in his reply.

'Over there,' the ghoul replied. He pointed to a little cottage near a stream on the outskirts of the castle grounds. 'Tell them to stay away from my castle. It's my castle,' he balled.

I walked over to the cottage, keeping an eye out for any sign of an angel. There didn't seem to be anyone about, but I knew that the angels were very mysterious and very fast, and that I might not be quick enough to notice their movements.

Eventually I just sat at the front door of the cottage and waited. I was waiting for a fairly long time when I heard a young girl yawning beside me.

She put a key in the lock and opened the door. She walked over to a table in the centre of the room and put her schoolbag down. She yawned again and then took off her coat.

'Mammy,' she shouted. 'Are you still in bed?'

'Yes,' came the reply. 'I've got a terrible sore head.'

'Take a tablet,' the girl shouted.

'I have,' mammy shouted. 'And I'm coming down to see you in a minute.'

Suddenly, as I was expecting mammy to arrive in with her daughter, a very large and powerful angel appeared at the front door.

'What do you want?' he asked.

'I'm a heaven dweller,' I said, 'and...'

'I know you are,' he said. 'I can tell.'

'I need to speak with an angel,' I said.

'Will I do?' the angel said. 'I'm an arch-angel.'

'Whaaaoow,' I said under my breath. I felt the need to be very polite. 'If it pleases you, I only want to ask you a question.'

'No need for formality,' he said pleasantly. 'Tell me your question.'

I thought for a moment about my question and I felt that it might sound rude. 'I don't know if it's a good idea to ask but I would like to know what your opinion would be of me seeking to repay a debt back on earth.'

'What kind of debt?' he asked straight away.

'To those who conspired to kill me,' I said nervously.

'Oh,' he said. 'That's quite a big debt. Why?'

'Because they have made my family tearful and hurt,' I replied.

'Well,' he said, 'there is only one rule involved in this kind of case, and I'm sure that you will agree to it, because I'm sure that you are extremely happy in heaven, and you wouldn't want anyone to get the mistaken impression that heaven is not a place worth being good for.'

'What's the rule?' I asked. He seemed reluctant to tell me.

'The rule is that, whatever you do in response to these killers' action, you must make people laugh,' he said finally.

'Laugh?' I wondered.

'Yes, laugh,' he said. 'That is the rule. You need to think very carefully about what you will do, but as long as you make people laugh, the angels don't mind. You needn't make the killers laugh, only those around them.'

Laugh! I was going to make them laugh all right!

Chapter Thirteen

I went back to Aideen, who was still with the other members of our group, and we sat down to talk about my dilemma.

We decided quickly that we would make it into an adventure for the entire group, and that I would return the favour whenever they needed something done back among the living.

Next day we set off for the hospital where I had been injected with an overdose of medication and, when we arrived there, we asked a heaven-dweller who had been watching over the place to advise us.

He told us that there had been two male nurses who had conspired with a doctor in order to carry out the foul deed. The nurses had apparently been on duty during the night in question and they had provided a cover and an alibi for the doctor.

The nurses hadn't really understood what was going to happen, but one was linked to the IRA and the other to the UDA, and they didn't mind that I had died for they were cold-hearted.

We decided that we would get the nurses first as they were on duty that day. We were told that they were rough, excitable men so we decided we would use that against them.

Towards the end of their shift, just when the other nurses were arriving to come on duty, and consequently just when there would be the largest audience possible, we got the smaller of the two men to steal a cigarette from the much bigger man's packet.

'Fucking pack it in,' the bigger man said.

'Why?' the smaller man said. 'What would you do?'

We gave them both almighty passions, and they were both steaming with anger.

'I'd kick your fucking teeth in,' the bigger man said.

'Fuck you,' the smaller man said, and he threw an almighty punch that landed straight on the bigger man's nose, breaking it. We had a former boxer on our team, who was an expert when it came to punching, and the little man was punching well above his weight.

'You broke my nose, you bastard,' the bigger man shouted, and he grabbed the little man by the lapels, lifted him up, and stuck his forehead into his face, breaking his nose too.

The blood was pouring from the wounds of the two men, and their faces had been altered extensively by the time they stopped fighting, a few minutes later.

'I don't know what came over me,' the big man said.

'I was out of order,' the little man said.

'You were both out of order,' the charge nurse said. 'You are both suspended, pending disciplinary proceedings, and I'll be seeing to it that you never work in this hospital again.'

Both of them hobbled out of the hospital with their tails metaphorically between their legs.

There was laughter in the hospital that night. The nurses on duty were delighted that they would no longer have to put up with the two thugs and malcontents. The patients were glad to see the back of the two nurses who bullied them and cajoled them at every opportunity. They had lost their jobs and everyone was happy. No-one was happier than I was that we were beginning to deal with the people who had caused my family so much grief.

'Two down,' I told the others, 'a doctor to come.'

'I can't wait,' Aideen said, and we all laughed.

The very doctor came on duty the next morning, and we decided that we needed to think very carefully about what we would do with him. The problem was that we could not think of anything that would make everybody laugh. Doctor were such serious people, who took themselves so seriously, that it was difficult to conceive of anything that would make everyone else laugh.

We decided eventually that we would intervene during his rounds that morning. So we waited for him to arrive at the chronic ward where Kevin was spending a little of his purgatory. We set things up there for the doctor when he would arrive.

When the doctor arrived there, we had everything planned. He was to mock the patients with all his might.

We inspired him to get into the mood by making him think that he was a great mimic, and that he could make people laugh with his imitations.

He began by mocking Mickey Joe, who had the habit of grumbling instead of talking.

'Go go gum tree,' he said, 'isn't that right Mickey Joe?' He thought that this was terribly funny, even though the nurses were staring at him, thinking that he was being lousy. We had convinced him that the nurses were finding his every act and syllable extremely funny.

Next he imitated Billy, who had a stutter when he said things that usually didn't entirely make sense.

'Gucci, Gucci, gooo-go-go-go,' he said and the nurses were absolutely furious with him. Of course, he believed that he was the funniest person on the planet. The doctor was really getting into the swing of things.

Next he saw Jimmy. Thinking that everyone was with him in his venture into extreme comedy, he pulled down his fly and pretended to expose himself by putting his finger out through his flies.

'Wiggly, wiggly, little worm,' he said, 'isn't that right, Jimmy?'

The nurses thought that he had gone bonkers, and so they began to laugh at him. This led in turn to him thinking that the laughter was overwhelming and powerful. He jumped up on a canteen table, pulled down his underpants at the front inside his trousers, and exposed himself.

This was where we came in with the *coup de grâce*. As he stood there laughing his head off, swinging his manhood round and round in a little circle, and thinking that he was the funniest man on the planet, the consultant walked in.

'Have you lost your mind, man?' the consultant shouted to his junior colleague.

Suddenly things didn't seem to be so funny anymore. The consultant had taken a dislike to him when he first arrived at the hospital, and so he was put on report pretty quickly, and was on a last warning when he was caught swinging his bit on the canteen table.

'You'll never work in medicine again,' he roared. 'You complete imbecile. Consider yourself suspended.'

Of course, we had been kind of expecting something from Kevin, our purgatory friend in the ward, and he didn't disappoint. Just as the doctor walked, head down, to the door, there was an almighty rustle of feet and a serious thump.

Suffice to say that the doctor left the ward on a stretcher, and Kevin's volunteer was trussed up on the floor until he calmed down.

Then all the smiling began, and then the laughing, and telling of colleagues in neighbouring wards. Everybody couldn't believe what had just happened.

'He went mad,' I heard one nurse say.

'He was swinging his dick,' another said.

Everyone was very amused by the mad doctor who had tried to mock the patients in front of a few nurses and a choir of heaven-dwellers. It was yet another beautiful moment.

Next we had to find the pathologist, Dr Connors, who had covered up the fact that I had died from poisoning on behalf of his friends. When we got to his office in Altnagelvin Hospital, near Gransha Hospital, he wasn't there. We asked a spirit who was watching over the hospital where he was, and she told us that he was carrying out an autopsy that morning.

'That could be an opportunity,' smiled Aideen wryly.

'It could be indeed,' I smiled in response, and we both laughed furiously. All of our group were laughing when we told them of what we had in mind.

We travelled down to the pathologist's laboratory then and watched over the situation for a while. Dr Connors was sipping a flask of whisky, which would make our task all the easier. He was an elderly, tallish man in his early sixties, with a bald head and grey hair.

When he was on his own, I got a couple of our group to go and watch the door in case anyone would enter. Then the fun began.

'You were a skinny so and so,' the pathologist said, speaking to the dead corpse, which he had a habit of doing.

'I was,' the corpse replied. 'I was on a diet,' she added.

'What?' Dr Connors shrieked, as he dropped his medical saw on the floor. 'What the hell is going on here?'

There were a few dead corpses lying on the trolleys next to the one the doctor was working on, and suddenly one of them sat up.

'You be careful with our girl, doctor,' he said. 'I don't want any scarring.'

'What the hell...?' Dr Connors roared. 'This can't be happening.'

He took the flask of whisky and threw it at the wall, thinking that he was being drugged.

Then another corpse rose up from her trolley. 'You killed John, you bad man. You killed our friend. You're a really bad man.'

'John who?' he asked.

'John, the young accountant,' she replied.

'I only helped some friends,' Dr Connors explained. 'I didn't kill him. I just covered up the killing.'

'You covered it up!' the three spirit shrieked together, and they moved forward in unison.

'Don't hurt me!' Dr Connors shouted.

'We're gonna eat you,' the three spirits roared.

'Help!' Dr Connors shouted, as he fell to the ground. 'They're going to eat me!'

We were almost finished. We couldn't think of anything else to do. Then someone had the idea of getting him to pretend to cut off his leg with the medical saw. It was enough to ensure that he never forgot that we were really with him.

Instead of waiting until he did it himself, Aideen grabbed the saw, as it lay on the ground beside him, and stuck it into his hand. He moved it slightly and it cut into his leg. He screamed and a little blood trickled down his leg.

We could hear people coming then, and we went back to our positions on the trolleys.

'Jesus!' screamed one of his colleagues. 'He's bleeding. Get the first aid kit. What happened?'

'The dead rose!' he shouted. 'They rose and they punished me for my terrible sin!'

'What?' the assistant asked. 'Dr Connor, are you losing your mind?'

'Yes,' Dr Connor said. 'I think I'm losing my mind. I need a good rest.'

'Well, doctor,' the assistant said, 'I know a place where you can get that kind of rest. I had no idea that you were so exhausted.'

'Where?' the doctor asked.

'A wee hospital near here,' his assistant said. 'We'll get the duty psychiatrist to have word with you.'

The duty psychiatrist arrived after about an hour, and by then the wound on Dr Connors' leg was washed and covered over.

'We found him here, trying to cut his leg off with a saw,' the assistant explained, 'and he was shouting that the corpses had come alive and punished him for his "sin".'

The psychiatrist smiled. 'Well,' she said, 'he's going to the right place now for a wee rest.'

Justice had been done. The pathologist had been punished, and the heaven dweller's had triumphed once again. Once the pathologist had gone, the laughing began in his office. His staff thought he had gone bonkers and were very happy since he had been a miserable boss.

We followed Dr Connors down to the hospital. We had no intention of doing him any more harm since we realised that it was going to be a long time before he got out of the psychiatric hospital. We just wanted to find out who the link was to Casey, the man who had broken my nose and whom all these men had been trying to help.

We interrogated Dr Connors when he was dosed up with medication, pretending to be the police. He thought that he was in real trouble, and wanted to plead guilty in return for a less severe sentence. So we asked him to name his accomplice. He genuinely didn't know the name of the doctor at the hospital who had carried out the overdose injection, but he told us of his old friend, a former student of St Columb's like Casey.

It was my old school too, but apparently Casey had influence there and was highly regarded in certain circles. He had friends there, friends who wouldn't be worth a roasted snowball in the bad times, but who were there for him when his star was rising.

The name of the accomplice was Padraig Donnellan, a mysterious man who had risen to prominence in the city with his businesses in the computer components sector, and whose star had been rising for several years. He had friends in all parts and he had called in favours to help Casey in his moment of need.

He was an altogether more serious challenge for our group, and we pondered the question as to whether he should be left to the angels who would carry out their business in a much more stringent manner. But we decided to give it a go, having been successful with the other characters.

Donnellan was the type of man who seemed to have everything sown up. His businesses were very profitable, and his factory was plush and modern. But he also had a new wife, his second, who seemed to us to be his weakness. She was in reality a woman who had married more for the money and prestige than for the love of her husband. She was ready to leave him at any moment since he knocked her about a bit.

Although his businesses were profitable, he had a cash flow problem at that time and was very much against, to say the very least, having to meet a divorce settlement. So we thought about it for a moment and each of the group gave their impression as to how he should be dealt with.

He was having a few friends around for drinks that night, so we decided on our plan and made ourselves comfortable in his beautiful home.

It was a time for hallucinating. The long and short of it was that Donnellan was having a fling with his friend and his friend's wife since he swung both ways. When his friend's wife went to the toilet upstairs, he approached her and moved her quickly into his bedroom for a quickie.

Aideen made his wife curious as to what was going on, and so she made her way upstairs. Just at the moment his wife was entering the bedroom, Donnellan looked up to find that it wasn't his friend's wife he was in bed with: it was his friend.

'Get out,' he shouted, just as his wife appeared round the door.

'You queer bastard,' she shouted, as a naked man emerged from their marital bed.

'It's not what you think,' Donnellan shouted. 'It was supposed to be his wife.'

'Divorce!' exclaimed Mrs Donnellan furiously. She then gathered her things and left for her mother's.

Donnellan was going to lose half his assets, and that meant that his cash flow problems would overwhelm him. He was going out of business.

Whenever the story was told around the town people laughed to think that this big butch man was being called a homosexual. We had succeeded again.

Chapter Fourteen

We spent that evening rolling around laughing while we listened intermittently to Donnellan telling what remained of his friends that he wasn't homosexual, and that he had really thought that he was shagging his best friend's wife when he was found in bed with his best friend.

I don't think anyone actually believed him. We roared with laughter every time he mentioned the word "straight". "I'm straight as a die," he would say, lying through his teeth.

Then there was Dr Connors. When we recalled how poor Dr Connors would feel now that we had given him reason to believe that he was losing his mind, we would laugh hysterically. It was extremely funny, and yet on a certain level it wasn't that funny at all. There he was, found trying to saw his leg off. He would get sectioned under the Mental Health Act for that, being a danger to himself, and it would be a long time before he would get out.

Of course, it wasn't funny in the sense that it needed to be done, that these people had conspired in a killing and in the covering up of a killing. These people had killed me, and I was happy that they were facing an appropriate "sentence". But it was sad that it had been necessary to do it at all.

To make myself feel better, I compared my family's suffering to the suffering these men would face. I was lost to my family, a burden that they would always feel, and these people had caused it by their actions.

I felt better when I looked at it like that. Then there was Casey himself.

I thought long and hard about what we could do to Casey. I was in a good position to get my friends to do something fairly outrageous to him. But an appropriate course just wouldn't come to mind.

For a long time I continued to think about the justice of the situation. Casey had apparently no knowledge of the cause of my death. It had been done as a favour to him but without his knowledge.

It seemed that he had merely complained that an injustice had been done to him, that there had been an attempt to "blackmail" him, and that he had wrongfully been reported to the police for investigation.

Of course, all his complaints were of a spurious nature. He had transacted for what he had got. He had simply asked for it. I was only defending my position, and when people do that, other people tend to get hurt.

In that sense, there was reversing of the fortunes of the night in August 1988 when all this began. That night he had broken my nose, his defence probably being that it was self-defence and, if he didn't defend himself then, he would have been in the same position, perhaps having his own nose broken.

I didn't accept that, even though it may have seemed that I acted out on the logic of that in the subsequent negotiations.

My view was and is that no violence would have happened on that night if it wasn't for Kevin Casey. He had been responsible for it occurring, solely responsible, and in subsequent discussions, near to the night in question, he had accepted that. For example, he had said that "it was a fair cop" when confronted with the possibility of charges being introduced when I discussed this with him the following day.

There is a tendency of victims of crime to come to think of their own role as blameworthy, but I would not have initiated violence that night in any circumstances, and thus I was not responsible for Casey's actions. They were the actions of a man not in control of his emotions. He was out of control, wallowing in hatred and envy.

He envied me for being in a good position to succeed John Hume, our MP, being working-class and extremely well-educated. He was jealous that I had what he wanted. Even his taking up of boxing during his university years may well have been meant to try to emulate things that I had done in the past.

His boxing had rendered my ability to strike back at him in a similar way impossible. Whatever about an eye for an eye, "a nose for a nose" was out since he showed me his flat nose, broken during his boxing days, during our discussions.

Nonetheless, his actions had such a serious impact on my life and health that they could not be treated with kid gloves, or with the kind of humour that had dominated our actions with his friends, and that they would be treated instead with extreme seriousness. The course that I chose was a most serious course.

I was left with no choice in relation to Kevin Casey. I had to forgive him, but with a warning that the angels would confront him with his actions of that August 1988 night, and of the subsequent months when he abdicated on his responsibility for his own actions, as soon as he attempted to enter the kingdom. That was a punishment of epic proportions.

With that I began to feel something strange happening to me yet again. The words "make things better" were repeated in my mind many times before I woke up in my hospital bed. I had been called to make things better.